Bill Duffy is a newspaperman, a real pro. photographer. He lives hard, drinks hard and he's tough – except where women are concerned. And when he finds himself with a ravishingly beautiful woman in her apartment very late one night, it takes all his willpower to resist – willpower, and a very mangled corpse which somehow fell down the elevator shaft. And that was only the beginning ...

Also by James Hadley Chase

James Hadley Chase

He Won't Need It Now

PANTHER
GRANADA PUBLISHING
London Toronto Sydney New York

Published by Granada Publishing Limited
in Panther Books 1975
Reprinted 1977

First published in Great Britain by
Rich & Cowan Ltd 1939
Copyright © James Hadley Chase 1939

Granada Publishing Limited
Frogmore, St Albans, Herts AL2 2NF
and
3 Upper James Street, London W1R 4BP
1221 Avenue of the Americas, New York, NY 10020 USA
117 York Street, Sydney, NSW 2000, Australia
100 Skyway Avenue, Toronto, Ontario, Canada M9W 3A6
Trio City, Coventry Street, Johannesburg 2001, South Africa
CML Centre, Queen & Wyndham, Auckland 1, New Zealand

Made and printed in Great Britain by
Cox & Wyman Ltd
London, Reading and Fakenham
Set in Intertype Plantin

For
JAMES WHITTAKER

Part One

IT BEGINS

CHAPTER ONE

The lounge of the Princess Hotel was crowded with stragglers, filling in time before going into dine. At the far end of the room, waiters hovered at the open doors of the restaurant, waiting patiently for someone to come on in and eat. It was just after seven o'clock, and the room was seething with movement as people pushed past small tables to greet friends, or shouted across, whichever way they felt.

William Duffy sat in a corner, drinking a Bacardi Crusta. The table before him held a number of bottles. The barman was a friend of his and let him mix his own drinks. There was a scowl on his face and he hadn't removed his hat. He just sat there drinking and smoking and scowling. Looking up suddenly, he saw Sam McGuire of the *Tribune* crawling by, muttering apologies as he lurched into small tables. Duffy reached out and touched Sam's cuff. Sam stopped at once.

'My God!' he said, 'I'm goin' blind or somethin'.'

'You ain't doing so badly,' Duffy said, looking him over. 'You ain't quite blind, but you're getting on.'

McGuire hooked a chair with the toe of his shoe and pulled it towards him. He folded himself down and grinned.

'You goin' on a bender?' he asked with interest, looking at the collection of bottles before him.

Duffy signalled the barman, who brought another glass. The barman looked the two of them over with a practised eye. 'Ain't goin' to overdo it, are yuh?' he asked in a pleading voice.

'Okay, don't you worry about us,' Duffy said, picking up the rum and pouring it into the shaker.

'I hope not, boss,' the barman took another long look and went back to his counter.

'Poor old George,' Sam sighed, 'he's forgotten us since he's moved in with the Big Shots. Listen Bill, make that a strong one. I guess I'm just about all in. If you notice a funny smell in a minute, go away, I shall've died on you.'

Carefully Duffy added the absinthe, squeezed a lime and spooned in some sugar. He chased some crushed ice round with the tongs before getting a grip, then he sealed the shaker and went to work.

McGuire lit a cigarette and pushed his hat on to the bridge of his nose. He looked at Duffy carefully while he handled the shaker. Duffy met his eye and grinned. 'Go on, I know what you're going to say.'

'It ain't true, is it?'

Duffy nodded his head and poured the shaker's contents into the two glasses. McGuire took his in his hand and rested his nose on the rim of the glass.

'Mi Gawd!' he said, 'you mean old Sourpuss has tossed you out?'

'Yeah, just like that.'

Sam sat back and groaned. 'What the hell—?'

'Listen,' Duffy said. 'Arkwright and me have been hating each other's guts for a long time. I never gave him a chance to bat me. Today I did. He'd been waiting for the chance and he grabbed it with two hands like a starving man would grab a dollar lunch. O boy! Did it make him feel good! He tossed me out so quickly, I'm still dizzy in the head.'

'But why, for the love of Mike?'

'I was young and innocent and you know how these things go. I didn't think he was that sort of a boy, and look, mother, what's happened now.'

'Skip the comedy.' Sam was sitting up with a fierce look on his broad face. 'Did you slip up on somethin'?'

'You know me, I don't slip on anything. Anyway, if I do, I cover it up all right. This was a frame. That heel Arkwright has been angling for an interview with Bernstein for weeks, and at

last he got it. You know how difficult Bernstein can be. He said
that art was out. Mind you, with a mug like that Yid's got on
him, I ain't surprised he was a bit touchy. Anyway, Arkwright
kept right at him until he gave way. I was sent along to get the
pictures. I reckoned I had a nice set until I got 'em in the bath,
then Mrs. Duffy's son had a shock. Those goddam' plates were
fogged, the whole lousy lot. Sabotage, that's what it was. Some
smart guy'd tampered with the stock. I tested the remaining
plates and they were all duds.' He paused for a pull at his glass.
Sam said nothing. His face was flushed and his foot tapped
against the leg of the table. Duffy knew he was getting mad.
'Well, I explained to Sourpuss and do you think he'd believe
me? Not likely! We exchanged a few words, and I guess I got
tough, so he ran me inside and they ran me outside.'

Sam helped himself to another Bacardi Crusta.

'This may put you in a spot,' he said thoughtfully. 'That
punk's got the ear of most Art Editors in town.'

'Sure, I know. Unreliable, fell down on a scoop!'

Duffy finished his drink and began to mix more Bacardis.
'What the hell,' he went on, 'it's my funeral anyway. Come on
in and feed with me.'

Sam climbed to his feet. He looked worried. 'Ain't possible,
soldier,' he said. 'I've got to get back and put in some more
sweat. Come over in the morning, will you? Alice's goin' to
be sore about this.'

Duffy nodded his head. 'I'll be over. Tell Alice not to lose
any sleep. I'll get somethin'.'

'Sure.' Sam clouted Duffy on the back, nearly jerking the
shaker out of his hands. 'Keep 'em bouncin', brother, keep 'em
bouncin'.'

When he had gone, Duffy finished the last of the Bacardis
and, feeling pleasantly drunk, sat back and considered his
future with optimism. He glanced over to the far end of the
room at the fat man who had been watching him all the evening. You can't go two hours or so with someone's eyes shifting
all over your face without feeling it, and Duffy had been
vaguely aware of intense scrutiny ever since the fat man had
come in.

Feeling more interested now, he wondered indifferently who

he was. In the past, he might have been unusually striking, but he had let himself go and he was running to fat in a big way. He had broad lumpy shoulders that might easily have carried a nasty punch, but he was getting thick in the middle, which told Duffy all he wanted to know. His face was big and fat, and his mouth turned down at the corners, giving him a dismal sneering look. His little eyes were restless and shifted about like black beads.

Duffy guessed he was on the wrong side of forty-five. He had dough all right. Not only were his clothes good, but they were cut right and he wore them right. There was an air of confidence that money brings; the look that tells you that the bank balance's fat.

Getting to his feet, Duffy began an unsteady journey to the restaurant, and he purposely made a detour so that he would pass the fat man's table. As he reached the table, the fat man climbed to his feet and stood waiting. Duffy stopped and looked him over. At close quarters he liked him a lot less.

'I'm Daniel Morgan,' the fat man said as if he were saying Rockefeller instead of Morgan. 'Mr. Duffy?'

Duffy squinted at him, astonished. 'Sure,' he said.

'Mr. Duffy, I want to talk to you. Will you dine with me?'

Duffy raised his eyebrows. He told himself that he wasn't spending his money, so he said that it was okay with him. Morgan led the way into the restaurant, and Duffy thought his guess that Morgan's wallet was well lined was a good one. He could tell by the way the waiters fawned on the fat man. He got a table in a corner, pretty secluded, and sat down. Duffy took a chair opposite him. Three waiters came bowing round them, and the wine waiter hovered outside the fringe. The *maître d'hôtel* came up smoothly as if he had been drawn along on wheels, and the other wops grouped themselves in a line at the back. Royal stuff, but even then Morgan wasn't satisfied. He wanted the chef. Well, of course he got the chef.

You either get a big kick out of tossing your weight around like that, or else you feel all hands and feet. Duffy felt all hands and feet.

The chef and Morgan got into a huddle with the bill of fare. He didn't ask Duffy what he wanted and Duffy was glad of that. He just kept talking in his deep harsh voice and the chef squeaked back at him in broken English until they had put a meal together that seemed to satisfy him. After they had done that, they got some elbow-room. Then Morgan remembered that Duffy was sitting opposite him.

'You'll excuse me for not asking you what you would like, but on these occasions I feel the choice of a good meal lies in the hands of the chef rather than in the hands of the diner. Consult the chef and you put him on his mettle. I think you will be satisfied.'

Duffy shrugged. He began to want another drink.

'I should like to confirm a few details,' Morgan went on; 'forgive me if I seem inquisitive, but my questions will eventually be to your advantage, so I must ask for your patience.'

This long-winded stuff gave Duffy a pain, but he hadn't had oysters for a couple of years, so he let himself go with them.

Morgan didn't seem to expect an answer, but went straight on. 'I believe you resigned from the *Tribune* this afternoon?' he said casually.

Duffy grinned. 'You're partly right there,' he said. 'I didn't resign, I was tossed out.'

'Arkwright is a difficult man.'

This bird seems to know all the answers. Duffy laid his oyster-fork on the plate and looked regretfully at the glistening shells. 'So what?' he said.

'You may find it difficult to get a job again.'

The soup and the sherry turned up then. Duffy looked at the sherry and then at Morgan. Morgan got it all right. 'Perhaps you would prefer Scotch?' he asked.

'These sissy drinks upset my guts,' Duffy said, apologetically.

The wine waiter was called and a bottle of Scotch materialized. Duffy felt he could cope with anything with that at his elbow. He gave himself a generous shot and dived into his soup again.

'As I was saying . . .' Morgan began.

Duffy raised his head. His eyes were hard. 'You seem to know a hell of a lot,' he said sharply, 'who told you—?'

Morgan waved his hand. 'Please,' he said, 'let me continue. I was saying, you will find another job difficult to get.'

Duffy laid his spoon down with a sharp clatter. 'You know, pal,' he said, 'a guy with my experience seldom stands in the bread-line. I've got a swell equipment, I know my job, and if the worst comes, I could set up a studio. I guess you're being mighty pleasant with your sympathy, but I ain't worryin' and I'd hate to have you worry for me.'

'I'm quite sure,' Morgan said, rather hastily, 'you'll get along all right, but I have a proposition that might be extremely useful to help you start that studio.'

'What is it?'

'Before we come to that, I wonder if you would enlighten me on a few technical points of your work?'

'Sure.' Duffy was getting bored with all this. 'What'd you want to know?'

'Would it be possible to get pictures of a person who is unaware of you, in ordinary lighting, in an ordinary room, who probably would be moving about. I want good pictures, not just anything.'

'It depends a lot on the room,' Duffy said, pouring some more Scotch in his glass and forgetting to put the water in after it. 'I wouldn't like to say without seeing the room. It depends so much on the walls, if they reflect the light. If you don't want real art, I could get you pictures all right. Pictures that would reproduce.'

'You could do that?'

'Yeah, that wouldn't be so hard.'

Morgan seemed satisfied with that and went off on another long-winded ramble about nothing at all. They went through the dinner without getting anywhere, and Duffy guessed Morgan was stalling until he had finished the meal. He was right, for when the coffee was served, Morgan lit a cigar for Duffy and one for himself and got down to business.

'This is a delicate situation,' he said, pursing his thick lips, and letting the heavy smoke slide, almost hiding his face. 'I don't want you to know too much about it. The less you know the better for both of us. My wife's being blackmailed and I want to help her out.'

Duffy grunted. He was surprised, but then you never knew what was coming to you, he told himself.

'Unfortunately my wife and I don't get on as well as we might.' Morgan fidgeted a little with his liqueur glass. 'We don't live together. However, that does not concern you. She is being blackmailed and I'm going to put a stop to it. She won't come to me for help, but that does not alter the situation. I want to catch this blackmailer with the goods. This is where you come in. I want you to get pictures of her giving this crook money, then I can crack down on him. It is no use trying to co-operate with Mrs. Morgan, she wouldn't want me to help her. I can get you into her apartment and you must do the rest. I shall pay you well.'

Duffy didn't like this. He thought there was a phoney smell that went with it. He shifted in his chair.

'This sounds like a job for a private dick,' he said, without any enthusiasm.

Morgan seemed to expect opposition. 'I want pictures,' he said with emphasis. 'To get them, I must employ an expert. You'll be wanting money pretty soon, and you're an expert. I think it fits, don't you?'

Duffy told himself that if he was going to pull this job, the dough had to be right.

'Now as to terms.' Morgan spread his big hands on the table-cloth and looked at them. 'I will give you five hundred dollars down, and a thousand dollars for every good picture you turn in.'

Duffy got his nerve back with a long drink. He was getting pretty high by this time, but he was still cautious. 'You must want those pictures mighty bad,' he said, thinking that he could do himself well with fifteen hundred bucks.

'I do,' Morgan said, 'I want them fast too. Will you do it?'

Duffy waved a hand. 'Take it easy,' he said, 'you're rushing me. I want to get this straight. You want me to go to your wife's apartment and take pictures of her and someone else and turn these pictures over to you, that right?'

Morgan was getting impatient, Duffy could see that, but he held himself in with an effort. 'That's right,' he said.

'What happens if she spots me and sends out the riot call?'

'She won't spot you,' Morgan said shortly. 'Let me give you the idea. She is crazy about music and she's rich enough to indulge herself. In her sitting-room she has a small organ loft. This loft's a kind of balcony about ten feet from the floor, looking into the room. It's reached by a special staircase and there is a back entrance to the staircase.'

Duffy reached for the Scotch, but Morgan put his hand on the bottle. 'Don't you think . . .?' he began, but Duffy took his hand away. He just lifted the fat man's hand and flung it back at him. His eyes looked annoyed. 'Listen,' he said tersely, 'if you think I'm gettin' drunk, forget it. When I want a drink, I have a drink, see?'

Morgan shrugged. His face was pale and he gently rubbed his wrist. 'Quite a grip you have there,' he said.

Duffy grinned. 'Sure,' he said. He poured the Scotch into the glass and swallowed it. 'Go on,' he said.

Morgan tapped on the table with his thick fingers. 'You see, my wife didn't want the musicians tramping through her room. They could come up the back entrance and get fixed without any fuss. All you have to do is to go up the stairs and lie on the floor in the dark and take photos of the room below. You can't be spotted.'

When he put it like that, Duffy thought it certainly seemed easy. At the same time, something told him that this set-up was not quite on the level. For one thing, Morgan didn't give him any confidence. On the other hand, the dough was good, and he was going to need it. He had another go at him.

'Let's look on the dark side,' he said; 'suppose she takes it into her head to play the organ and finds me up there, what then?'

Morgan shrugged his fat shoulders. 'There's no other way up to the loft, so all you have to do is to slip the bolt. Once you're there, you're safe.' He took out his wallet and pushed five one-hundred-dollar bills over the table. 'Besides,' he said with a little oily smile, 'you surely expect to earn this money and not just have it given you.'

Duffy reached over and took the bills. He shoved them in his inside pocket. 'Okay,' he said, 'when do I start?'

Morgan pulled out a gold watch and glanced at it. Duffy

noticed that his hand shook a little. 'It's just after ten now,' he said, 'you've got to get your equipment, and then go to the house. I think we could start now.'

Duffy got to his feet and pushed back the chair with his legs.

Morgan looked at him and said quietly, 'I want to impress on you that this is important—'

Duffy raised his hand. 'Skip it,' he said, 'you don't have to tell me all that again. A thousand bucks a picture is more than important to me.'

Morgan climbed out of his chair. 'You can do quite a bit with money like that,' he said.

Duffy said, 'You're telling me.'

CHAPTER TWO

Morgan had been quite right. The whole set-up was easy. Duffy sat on his heels in the organ loft and felt hilariously at home. The small camera hung round his neck by a strap and the lighting of the room gave him no misgivings. He was going to make some money, he told himself. The organ loft was just as Morgan had described. It had an uninterrupted view of the room below and it was partly screened by heavy magenta curtains. Duffy had bolted himself in, and with the help of a pint of Scotch that he had brought with him, his nerves were calm and he could take a professional interest in his work.

He set the camera, using a big stop and a fairly fast shutter. Then he settled himself down to wait. Morgan had driven him to his apartment to collect his equipment and then had driven him to the back entrance of the loft. Morgan seemed to have had the whole thing planned carefully and it ran on oiled wheels. He had arranged to meet Duffy at the Princess bar that night, and Morgan was prepared to wait until he came.

Duffy looked down at the room with appreciation. It was a pretty swell joint, he told himself. The decoration was in magenta and cream. A cream pile carpet on the floor, and the large leather chairs, half cream and half magenta, gave the room a smart modern appearance. Duffy thought he'd like to have a place like this for his own.

He glanced at his wrist-watch. It was getting on for midnight. He wished that he could smoke, but he thought that that would be too risky. He wondered how long he had to wait. Just then the door below opened and a woman walked in hurriedly. She crossed the room and disappeared through another door. She had moved so quickly that Duffy hadn't had a chance to see what she was like. He cautiously spread himself on the floor, so that he was lying full length, his elbows supporting his arms as he swung the camera into position. He found that he could aim the camera through the narrow slots of the balcony, and he knew that he was completely hidden from the room below. He made himself comfortable by taking out a pint bottle of Scotch from his pocket, which was digging into him, then he settled down to wait.

A quarter of an hour dragged past, and he began to get fidgety, but suddenly he heard a faint whirr of an electric bell. He stiffened and looked towards the door expectantly. The woman came out and crossed the room. He could see her now, and he thought, 'O boy! O boy!' She was tall and slender. The pale green wrap of heavy silk which she had changed into set her figure off sharply. Duffy appreciated his private view. He admired her skin, which was pale and lovely, and he told himself that a dame with eyes as large as hers was a menace to weak men. He felt mighty weak himself towards her. Her scarlet lips promised passion, and he thought the red-gold hair was just the right finish to a mighty swell job. He thought Morgan showed a nice taste in women, but at the same time he wondered how a dame like that could have fallen for Morgan in the first place. It didn't surprise him in the least that she had given Morgan the air.

He watched her go to the door, and when she came back into the room again a man followed her closely. Duffy looked with interest at him. He was short and slight, with dark wavy hair. He seemed nervous and his face was unusually pale. The woman sat on the arm of a chair, quite close to a lamp standard. Duffy noted that the light fell directly on her. He focused his camera and gently pressed the release. The shutter slid with a faint click and Duffy pulled the trigger-like film-changer.

The man below said in a low voice, 'You got it?'

When she spoke, her voice came drifting up to Duffy in a soft cadence. She had that rather breathless voice with a very faint huskiness that make most men interested. Duffy was more than interested.

She said, 'I have the money.' She spoke with contempt, and the man squirmed under her gaze. 'Did you bring the stuff?'

'I want the dough first,' he said; 'make it snappy, lady, it ain't too healthy for me being here.'

Again she looked at him, then turning to the table she pulled out a drawer. Duffy saw her take out a thick wad of greenbacks. He again pressed the release. The faint click of the shutter seemed to roar in his ears. Down below, they noticed nothing. He saw the woman give the money and then the man, in his turn, hand over a small parcel. Duffy fired off his camera, pulling the film-changer rapidly, intent on what was happening below him. Then he lowered the camera, satisfied that he had got what he wanted. He reckoned he had at least twenty photos, and most of those would be nice ones. He calculated that five thousand bucks would be his by the morning, and he groped on the floor for the Scotch. He still kept his eye on the two in the room, but nothing was happening to get excited about, and he felt that a drink would help him along. At the back of his brain he was trying to place the short man down there in the room. He had seen him somewhere, but where it was, for the moment, escaped him.

The man was moving to the door now. He sidled like a crab, watching the red-headed woman closely. She followed him out of Duffy's sight and after a short delay she came back again. Duffy watched her. She relaxed into one of the chairs. Her green wrap parted and Duffy could see her long white legs. He raised himself slowly, so that he could see better. This dame was certainly a honey. He wondered if she had anything on under that wrap. The thought disturbed him, and he nearly wrenched his neck muscles trying to see more of her. He felt dispirited leaving her all on her own, but then, Morgan was waiting and so was the dough. He guessed that he wouldn't get to the first base with this dame without dough, and to get it he had to leave her. He rose quietly to his feet and took a step back. *Something hard dug him in the back.*

'Grab a little air, lug,' said a voice in his ear.

In the ordinary run of things, Duffy's nerves were pretty sound, but this nearly ruined his heart. He felt his long limbs quiver with shock, and he raised his hands quickly.

'Take it easy,' went on the voice, 'don't start anything.'

Duffy turned his head very slowly and looked over his shoulder. Standing behind him was a broad-shouldered man, wearing a black Fedora, pulled down low. In spite of Duffy's usual nonchalance, he felt his short hairs on his nape bristle. There was something utterly repulsive in the hard white face behind him. It gave Duffy the same feeling he might have got if he turned over a rotten log that had been lying in long grass for some time, and suddenly seen the foul things the log hid. The scurry of beetles and ants, the brown dead grass, and the white fungi, and particularly the long white slug that squirmed away from the sunlight. Down below he heard a door shut, and he guessed that the woman had left the room. Keeping his hands raised, he said, 'For the love of Mike, where did they find you?'

The man's eyes were almost closed, but the light in the room was sufficient for Duffy to see that they were mean and hard. He dug the gun into Duffy hard.

'Stand still,' he said again. His voice was hoarse as if he smoked too much. He put out a hand and snatched the camera hanging from Duffy's neck. The strap snapped, jerking Duffy's head forward.

'Hi!' Duffy said, in alarm. 'You ain't pinching my outfit?'

'Shaddap,' the man snarled at him.

A violent rage consumed Duffy. 'A frame-up huh?' he snorted. 'Mr. Sonofabitch Morgan wants his pictures for nothing?'

'If you don't stop yappin', I'll blast your guts,' the other rasped. 'What the hell do you think you're doin' in here?'

Duffy began to lower his hands, but the gun dug into him again. 'Listen,' he said, 'I'm just doin' a job of work. Come to that, what about yourself?' All the time he was speaking, he was wondering if this tough would shoot him. He began to think he was in a bit of a spot.

'I guess we'll go for a little walk,' the other said. There was a threat in his voice, but he took a step back, taking the gun from Duffy's side. Duffy didn't hesitate. He took a deep breath and suddenly kicked back with his heel. He hoped to connect with the other's leg. Maybe splinter his shinbone for him but his leg shot back meeting nothing, and before he could save himself he toppled over the low balcony and crashed into the room below.

He came down on his hands, breaking his fall by sliding a little on the carpet. For a moment the shock did things to him, then he sat up.

A door opened and he looked up gingerly, wondering if his brain had broken loose from its moorings. The red-head was standing there. She crossed her arms over her breasts and screamed. A breathless little scream that made Duffy want to put his arms round her and soothe her; not perhaps quite the same way as a mother might soothe her hurt child, but along those lines. When he saw the .25 in her hand he changed his mind.

Women with guns made him nervous. He could never believe that they were safe with them. Before now, a woman had held him up with a gun. He remembered one particularly irate blonde who had been so mad with him that she had squeezed the trigger a little too hard. The thought made him sweat a little, and he sat on the floor very still, giving her no cause for alarm.

Her eyes were large and scared, and her red lips were parted, showing her white even teeth. Duffy thought she was pretty good.

'Who . . . who are you?' she stammered breathlessly.

'Lady,' he said, holding his head in his hands, 'I'm asking myself the same question.'

'What are you doing here?'

Duffy looked at her through laced fingers. 'Would you mind very much putting that rod away? I've just fallen out of that loft and my nerves won't stand any more.'

'Will you tell me what you are doing here?' She was getting her nerve back, and her voice was steady.

'For the love of Mike don't start gettin' tough,' he pleaded, 'take a look at that hoodlum up there before you get that way.'

She looked frightened again. 'Is there anyone else up there?'

Duffy laughed shortly. 'I should say so,' he said, rubbing the back of his head gingerly, 'he's just tossed me out, so I should know.'

She took a step back hastily and looked up into the loft, then she shook her head. 'There's no one there.'

Duffy groaned. 'The so-and-so's pinched my camera,' he said wearily. 'Do you mind if I get up? There's a draught round here that ain't doing me much good.'

'I think you had better stay where you are,' she said firmly. She held the gun steady as she reached for the telephone.

'Don't do that,' Duffy said in alarm, 'you ain't calling the cops, are you?'

'Isn't that what I ought to do?' she asked, her hand hesitating on the receiver.

'Listen, Mrs. Morgan, I can explain everything. It's all a big mistake,' Duffy said; then he pondered and went on, 'I've heard that crack before. My God! I must be losing my grip or some-thin'.'

She lowered the gun in her astonishment. 'Why do you call me that?' she asked quickly.

Duffy stiffened a little. 'Ain't you Mrs. Morgan?'

'No, of course not.'

He scrambled to his feet and waved his hands at her as she jerked up the gun. 'Okay, okay, skip it,' he said impatiently, 'this is important. Who are you?'

She tapped her foot on the floor. 'What *is* this?'

'I'll tell you what this is,' Duffy said furiously, 'I've been taken for a ride. You've got to get this straight. Listen, Toots, I'm Duffy of the *Tribune*. Some guy who called himself Morgan spun me a yarn that you were his wife and you were being blackmailed. He wanted me to take photos of the crook who was putting the screws on you. I fell for this guff and came up to the hen-roost here and took photos of you and the guy you slipped the money to. Just as I am reaching for my hat and calling it a nice day's work, some thug hops up, pinches my camera, and heaves me out on my neck. You tell me you ain't Mrs. Morgan. In your own interests you'd better tell me who you are.'

She stared at him and then said finally, 'I think you must be mad.'

'Use your head,' Duffy was getting impatient, 'can't you see that you're in a spot? Morgan wanted a photo of you with this other guy and he's got it. Ask yourself why.'

She still stared at him and shook her head. 'I don't understand . . . I don't believe . . .'

He slid across to her in one movement and pushed the gun away. 'For Krizake,' he said roughly, 'will you listen to me? Who was the guy you gave that money to?'

His urgency touched her and she said quickly, 'I don't know. I think his name's Cattley . . .'

Duffy stepped back. 'Cattley . . . of course. By heck! I *must* be losing my grip. Cattley . . .' He swung round on her. 'What the hell are you doing with a rat like Cattley?'

Her eyebrows came together. 'Will you stop asking me questions—?' she began.

'Listen, baby.' Duffy came close to her. His voice had a sharp edge to it. 'Cattley's got a name that stinks in this town. Everyone knows him. Cattley the pimp. Cattley the dope. Cattley the slaver. I tell you he's poison to dames like you. You . . . you've let yourself be photographed with him . . . and someone's got those photos. Does that mean anything to you?'

'But—' she stopped and he saw she had gone pale.

'Yeah! That's made you think. Sit down and tell me quick. Make it snappy; I've got things to do.'

She turned on him suddenly with furious eyes. 'You started this,' she stormed at him. 'If it hadn't been for you—'

'Forget it!' he snapped at her. 'I'm getting those pictures back all right. But you've got to wise me up a hell of a lot before I do.'

The flash of temper was gone almost before it started. She sat down limply on the large settee and tossed the gun on the table. Duffy winced a little. Women were hell when it came to handling guns. He took a quick glance and saw that the safety catch was still down.

'Now come on, come on, let's get down to it,' he said, sitting on the edge of the table. 'What's your name?'

'Annabel English,' she said, twisting her hands in her lap.

'What are you? Just a little dame with plenty of dough, running round lookin' for a good time?'

She nodded. Duffy lit a cigarette. 'Yeah I bet you are, and I bet you have a pretty nice time of it. What's this Cattley to you?'

Her face flushed and she hesitated. 'I . . . I asked him to get material on the . . . the underworld. . . .' She stopped. The colour in her face was deep.

Duffy groaned. 'For the love of Mike, don't tell me you're writing a book or something,' he pleaded; 'a Society-dame-looks-on-the-underworld stuff?'

'I thought it would be amusing,' she said. 'It's about the White Slave traffic . . .'

He threw up his hands. 'So you thought you would write a book on the White Slave traffic, did you?' he said, dragging smoke into his lungs and letting it drift from his nostrils. 'And you've to pick on the worst hoodlum in town to help you. Well, I reckon you'd better change your ideas and write a book on blackmail. You're going to get a grandstand seat in this racket, and if you ain't careful you're going to pay plenty.'

She looked up swiftly, her face resentful. 'What am I to do?'

Duffy slid off the table. 'You ain't doing a thing at the moment. I'm getting that camera back. That's the first thing.'

He walked over to the telephone. 'Take a look in the book and see if you can find Daniel Morgan in it,' he said, spinning the dial. She got to her feet and began to rustle through the directory. While he was waiting for the line to connect he let his eye run over her as she leant forward over the table. 'Annabel English,' he thought. 'A swell name and a nice little job.'

A sharp metallic voice snapped in his ear, '*Tribune* here, what department do you know?'

'H'yah, Mabel,' he said. 'Dinny in?'

'Hold on an' I'll put you through.'

McGuire came on the line. 'Hello, pal,' he said. Duffy thought he sounded a little drunk.

'Listen, soldier,' Duffy said, keeping an edge on his voice.

'This is important. Will you meet me at the Princess Hotel right away?'

McGuire groaned. 'Aw, what you think I am? I'm goin' home. Listen bozo, what'll Alice say? I ain't been home all this week.'

Duffy was certain McGuire was drunk. 'I'll fix Alice,' he said. 'Get going and make it fast.' He hung up as McGuire began to protest again.

Annabel English said, 'There are ten Daniel Morgans in the book.'

'That's okay,' Duffy returned. 'I'll find him.' He walked over to her. 'Now you forget about this ... leave it to me. I'll give you a ring tomorrow and let you know how it went.' He paused, looking into her blue smoky eyes. 'You all alone here?'

She nodded. 'I sent my maid out for the evening. I didn't want her to see Cattley—'

'You ain't scared?'

'Why should I be?' She looked startled.

Duffy shrugged his shoulders. 'Why, I just thought ...' He suddenly grinned at her. 'If I get that camera, shall I come back an' see you tonight?'

Her eyes laughed at him, but her face was quite serious as she shook her head. 'I shan't be alone—'

'Who's your boy friend ...?'

She walked slowly to the door. He could see her smooth muscles moving under the green wrap. He knew that she hadn't anything on under that. She looked over her shoulder. 'I think you had better go now,' she said, 'I've heard that you news-papermen get funny ideas when you're alone with girls.'

Duffy looked round for his hat and found it near the settee. 'Well, what of it?' he said, walking to the door. They stood quite close, facing each other. 'What the hell's a girl got to beef about if he does? Ain't that a compliment to the girl, anyway? By heck! I can guess how they'd feel if we didn't get that way sometimes!'

She opened the door and he walked past her. Standing in the doorway, he faced her again. 'Well, good night, Toots,' he said with his wide grin, 'sleep easy ... I'm goin' to do things for you.'

Pushing the door slowly to, she kept his eyes watching her. Then when the door was nearly shut she leaned forward. 'Did you say your name was Duffy?'

'Yeah!'

'Anything else?'

'Bill Duffy, if you like.'

'It's a nice name.' She leant against the doorway, the door pulled against her fat hip.

Duffy stood there, putting his personality over on a short wave. 'It's an old family name,' he said modestly and grinned.

She raised her eyebrows. 'So?'

Duffy moved a little her way until he leant against the wall, touching her shoulder. 'We Duffys go for red-heads,' he said.

She raised her chin. Her lips invited his. 'Yes?' she said.

He touched her lips with his. A long green arm slid round his neck and pulled his head down. She did not close her eyes and when he looked into them he tried to jerk his head away, but she held him hard. Stormy, hungry wild eyes she had. He stood there, his mouth crushed on hers, startled by her fierceness. She suddenly drove her teeth into his top lip. The pain stung him, and he pushed her away violently, starting back with an angry oath. She stood looking at him, her red-gold hair wild, and her eyes big and dark, stormy with passion. She took a step back and slammed the door in his face.

Duffy stood there, dabbing his lip with his handkerchief. 'That dame's gonna let herself go one day,' he said to himself, 'and when she does, she's going to make a meal of someone.'

He walked slowly to the elevator and pressed the button. His lip was beginning to swell already. He stood before the grille, waiting for the elevator to come up. 'My God,' he thought, 'what a hell of a night.'

As the elevator came up slowly he saw, lying on the roof, the mangled body of a man. He watched the roof glide past him, carrying its grisly burden, then the empty cage came to rest at his floor.

He stood very still, feeling the sweat start out all over him. He said, 'Well, well,' for something better to say, then he walked back to the flat and hammered on the door.

CHAPTER THREE

She didn't come to the door at first. It was only by keeping his thumb on the buzzer, while the minutes ticked by, that Duffy got her to come at all. When she did come, she had the door on the chain. Duffy thought it was a hell of a time to start playing around with door-chains, but he let it drift with the current.

She started to close the door when she saw who it was, but Duffy got the toe of his shoe in first.

'Listen, bright girl,' he said, 'open up, and be your age. You've got a corpse on your hands right outside.'

'I honestly believe you're as mad as a coon,' she said breathlessly, 'or very, very drunk.'

Duffy leant his weight against the door, his face pressed against the small opening. 'Cattley's on the roof of the elevator. First glance, I'd say it was in the basement when he hit it.'

He saw her eyes widen, and then she giggled. He'd have forgiven her if she had screamed, or even passed out, but the giggle made him mad. He took a step back.

'That suits me, if that's the way you want it.'

She pushed the door to, slipped the chain, then opened the door and stepped into the corridor.

'Wait,' she said, putting her hand on his sleeve. Her hand looked white against his dark suit.

'Someone'll want this elevator in a moment and then things are going to happen.'

'Is he really . . . I mean, you're not just saying this to scare me?'

He got in the elevator, slid the grille and pressed the down button. He let the elevator sink half-way, then broke the current by opening the grille. He climbed out with a struggle, leaving the cage between floors.

'Does that look like a bedtime story?'

She peered at Cattley, not moving her body, but just craning her neck. One of her hands went to her mouth. 'Is he dead?'

'Do you think he's catching some sleep up? Look at him, baby, look at his arms and legs. Could you sleep like that?'

She turned on him angrily. 'Well, do something about it,' she said.

He pushed his hat to the back of his head. 'I'm beginning to wonder if you're as dumb as you seem to be. You wouldn't be dumber than a hophead, the way that brain of yours works. Do something about it? Well, what you want me to do? Send for the cops? Call an ambulance? What?'

She raised both hands and pushed her hair off her ears. She did it unconsciously. 'But you must know what to do,' she said.

Duffy stood looking at Cattley with a faint grimace, then he went over and took hold of him. He gripped his arm and shoulder. It gave him quite a turn when the arm bent back at the elbow. There were a very few bones in one piece with this guy. He pulled and slid Cattley off the roof and let him as gently as he could on to the floor. Cattley's legs folded up, but not at the knees, they folded up in the middle of his shins. Duffy felt himself sweating. Putting his hands under Cattley's shoulders, he dragged him into the flat and laid him out in the hall.

'What are you bringing him in here for?' Her voice was pitched half a note higher.

'Don't talk now,' he said, looking with disgust at the blood on his hands. 'This guy's going to make a mess in your joint, but it's better than making a mess of you.'

He walked back to the lift and inspected the roof. The woodwork was smeared with blood.

'Get me a wet towel,' he said.

She went into the apartment, carefully walking round Cattley. He stood by the lift watching her. She'd got a good nerve, he told himself. She came back again with a wet hand-towel. He took it from her and carefully mopped off the bloodstains. Then he wiped his hands on the towel and folded it neatly. He walked into her apartment and put the towel on Cattley's chest. She followed him in, again skirting Cattley, drawing her green wrap close to her.

'Will you see if he's got the money on him still?' she said.

Duffy looked at her hard.

'What makes you think the money ain't there?'

'It's the way I said it. I meant will you get the money from him.'

Duffy grimaced. 'I hate handling this bird. He's brittle.'

She came and stood close to him, looking down at Cattley. 'Isn't he going to get stiff soon?' she said. 'Hadn't you better straighten him out a little before he gets that way?'

Duffy said, 'For God's sake,' but he knelt down and cautiously pulled on Cattley's legs. One of his shin-bones poked up through his trousers leg. Duffy got up and looked round the hall. He went over to the coat-rack and selected a walking-stick. Then he came back to Cattley and put the ferrule of the stick on the shin-bone and pressed. The leg straightened, and he did the same with the other one.

His face was a little yellow, and sweat glistened on his top lip. Cattley was making him feel a little sick. He hooked the handle of the stick round Cattley's arm and put his foot against Cattley's body then he pulled gently. The arm came out from under Cattley like a limp draught-preventer.

Cattley's head lay on his right shoulder. The skin round the neck had split a little. Duffy straightened the head too with the stick.

'Want me to cross his hands?' he said for something to say. All the time he was fixing Cattley, she stood at his elbow and watched. Then she said, 'Get the money.'

Duffy looked at her, his eyes narrowed. 'Leave the money where it is,' he said shortly, 'get me a drink.'

She went into the sitting-room and he followed her. He suddenly found that he was still holding the walking-stick. It had blood-smears on it. He went and put it beside Cattley. Then he walked back into the sitting-room again.

She stood by the table, fixing a Scotch. He took the glass from her before she could add a Seltzer and tossed the liquor down his throat. It was good Scotch. Silky and full of body, with no raw bite in it. He felt it in his belly, a round little knot of warmth. He took the bottle from the table and poured himself another glass.

'Did you kill him?' he said, looking at her over the top of the glass.

She spread her hands across her breasts, standing very quiet for a moment, then she said, 'Was he killed?'

Duffy took another pull at his glass. 'Use your head,' he said shortly, 'how could he have fallen down the shaft? He wasn't drunk, was he? Think a moment. He goes out of your apartment. The elevator is standing on the ground floor. He opens the grille to look at it, then he feels giddy and falls down. They wouldn't pass it in a nut factory.'

She was going white again and she sat on the edge of the table. Her wrap fell open, showing her knees, but neither of them bothered with that.

'This is the way it went. Cattley goes out to the elevator and is smacked on the dome, then he is tossed down the shaft. That makes sense.' Duffy put the glass down on the table and lit a cigarette. 'You ain't answered my question. Did you kill him?'

'No,' she said.

'There's only one person who's going to believe that,' Duffy said, 'and that's you.'

She raised her head. Her big eyes were frightened now. 'You don't think I killed him?' she said; her words ran into each other.

'Can't you see what a spot you're in?' he asked patiently. 'Look, let me wise you up. Cattley calls on you to sell you something. You say it's material for a book; okay, it's material for a book. You show him the door and then, there he is on the elevator roof smashed to bits.'

'That doesn't prove that I killed him,' she said breathlessly.

Duffy shrugged. 'It helps,' he said; 'let me have a look at that material he sold you.'

She slid off the table and walked into her bedroom. Duffy sat down in an armchair. He gave her a few minutes, then he called, 'I guess the killer pinched it.'

She came out of the bedroom, her face white. She stood in the doorway, one hand at her throat, the other gripping the door-handle.

'I . . . I can't find it,' she whispered.

Duffy pursed his lips. 'I bet you can't,' he said. Then he got to his feet. He walked over to her and took both her elbows in his hands, he drew her towards him. 'You're a goddam silly little loon,' he said evenly, 'you think you can play this out on your own. Well, you can't. You've put on the thinnest act I've ever struck. That writing a book on the underworld went out with the Ark. Get wise to yourself, red-head.'

She drew away from him. 'What are you going to do?' she asked, her voice a little flat and toneless.

Duffy scratched his head. 'This is a hell of a night,' he said, then he stood very still, his fingers spread through his hair. 'I wonder . . .' he broke off, looking at Annabel. 'It looks to me that Morgan wants you to take the rap for Cattley's murder,' he said, speaking rapidly, 'it fits, by God!' He was getting quite excited. 'Listen, baby, how's this for a theory? Morgan gets me to photograph you and Cattley. Cattley gets smacked down by one of Morgan's mob just outside your door and tossed down the shaft. I get my camera pinched containing the photos. All Morgan has to do is to threaten to turn the pictures over to the cops for you to dive into your deposit account and fork out plenty.'

Annabel was scarcely breathing. 'Will you help me?'

Duffy said, 'I can't help myself, can I?'

'You're being nice, aren't you?'

'Nice, hell! I took the photos, didn't I? I've got to do something to square that.'

She dropped into the arm-chair, and held her hand over her eyes. Duffy looked at her and then fetched another glass from the wagon. He poured in three fingers of Scotch and then filled his own glass. He came over to her. 'Can you drink this stuff?' he said.

She took the glass from him. 'I don't want it,' she said.

'You'd better get a little drunk,' he said, 'you've got a nasty job on your hands.'

She looked at him and he jerked his head at the door. 'I guess we've got to get rid of Cattley.'

She said, 'Can't you do it?'

He grinned mirthlessly. 'You're in on this, too, sister,' he said. 'I'm helping you, but I ain't taking any rap.'

She drank the whisky neat and he gave her a cigarette.

'In a couple of hours that bird's going to get as stiff as a board. I guess he won't be too nice to handle like that. Now, we could pack him in a bag without much fuss.'

She shuddered.

'It beats me where the hell we're going to plant him.' Duffy began to pace the floor. 'He's got to remain planted and he ain't going to be found. As soon as they turn him up, then those photos will come into the market. It's the only way we can beat their game.'

He looked at her. 'Go and get dressed,' he said.

She got out of the chair and moved over to the bedroom. 'Give me a trunk, if you've got one,' he said.

She paused. 'There's one in here,' she said.

He followed her into the bedroom. She pointed to a large wall cupboard and he opened the door. In the corner was a small black cabin trunk. It was covered with labels. There seemed to be every hotel under the sun advertised on its black shiny sides. He looked at it and then he said, 'You've got about.' She didn't say anything. He hauled the trunk out and dragged it into the sitting-room.

'You got a sheet of mackintosh that I could wrap him in?' he called.

She came to the door. 'Mackintosh?'

'He's going to mess this trunk without it.'

She went across to another door and disappeared. He could hear her rummaging about, then she came out with a large luggage wrap. 'Will this do?'

'Yeah.' He took it from her.

'Don't say "yeah",' she said.

He stood holding the mackintosh. 'What's it to you?'

'It's tough.'

He stood staring at her. 'Suppose it is tough,' he said, 'isn't this a hell of a time to start a crack like that?'

'Do you think so?'

He let the luggage wrap slide out of his hands on to the floor. He could see her eyes were completely blank. She was hissing a little through her teeth. She fumbled with the girdle round her waist until she had it undone. The green wrap fell open and he saw she was naked. She stood a little on her toes, her hands clenched at her sides.

'Take me,' she said, her voice just above a whisper, 'take me, take me, take me.'

Duffy smacked her face. He could see the marks of his fingers on her white skin. Then he smacked her face again. She blinked twice. Her eyes became human again, and she stood looking at him, a surprised and frightened look on her face.

'Get dressed,' Duffy said thickly. He could only think of Cattley.

She turned away from him and walked limply into the bed-room, then she shut the door.

Duffy blotted his face with his handkerchief. He picked up the mackintosh sheet and walked into the hall. All the time he was telling himself what a sweet spot he had got himself into. It was bad enough to have to handle Cattley in the state he was in, but a dame as screwy as Annabel flattened him. He looked at Cattley in disgust. 'If you weren't going to stiffen on me, I'd be having fun right now,' he said viciously.

He spread the sheet flat by Cattley's side, then he picked up the walking-stick and hooked hold of Cattley's armpit. He couldn't quite bring himself to touch him with his hands. With a little manoeuvring he rolled him on to the sheet. Then he knelt down and made a neat parcel of the body.

By the time he had done that he felt so low that he went back into the sitting-room and gave himself another shot of Scotch. His legs were feeling light, and he guessed he was getting pretty high. His head was clear, and he felt just reckless enough to go on with it.

He poured out a stiff dose in Annabel's glass and went into the bedroom. When he got in the room, he nearly dropped the whisky. She was lying on her side on the bed. She was in her birthday suit, and it was a pretty good birthday suit at that.

He put the glass on the small table by the bed, and then he backed out of the room. There was only one driving thought in his mind. He had to plant Cattley before his muscles went like a board. Once he got that way, Duffy knew he'd be sunk.

He went into the kitchen and flicked on the light. The kitchen was large, with white tiles half-way up the walls, and yellow varnished paint on the other half. The floor was covered with large black and white checks. He thought it was a swell kitchen. He hunted about until he found a length of cord, then he went back to Cattley, lying snug in his parcel. He knelt down and made the parcel secure with the cord. Then he walked back to the sitting-room and dragged the trunk into the hall and wedged Cattley into it.

Half-way through he had to stop and sit on a chair. There was no resistance in the parcel at all. Cattley was just pulp. He sat there staring at the trunk and at the bulge of the mackintosh, that overlapped the sides of the trunk. Then he got up and wedged the overlapping parts in with the stick. The lid wouldn't quite close, so he stood on it. That made him feel bad, but he got the locks fastened somehow.

He took out his handkerchief and wiped off his palms and patted his face.

While he was standing there Annabel came out of the bedroom. She was wearing a black skirt, a white silk blouse, and a black three-quarter coat. She held a pair of magpie gauntlets in her hand. She moved slowly, with just a little sway on. He could see that the whisky was hitting her.

She peered at him

'He's packed up,' he said harshly.

She said nothing, but he was surprised to see how her eyes hated him. He thought about it for a moment, then agreed that she had reason to be sore.

'I never was good with a corpse lying around,' he said.

She ignored that and stood, her head turned away from him, by the table. 'What now?' she said.

'Can you get your car?'

'The garage is in the basement.'

Duffy went outside and pressed the buzzer for the elevator. It came up steadily and he found himself looking for more corpses. There weren't any. He slid the grille, then walked into the apartment. She made no move to help him drag the trunk into the cage. It was heavy, but he did it all right.

She followed him into the elevator and they both stood beside the trunk. Neither of them looked at it. He put his thumb on the basement button and the cage sank. He counted the floors as they went by. By the time they got to the basement, he counted twelve. He thought Cattley was lucky to have any skin left at all.

The attendant came up with a run. He was a little runt, with wire-like black hair. When he saw Annabel he nearly fell over himself. He looked just like an excited puppy.

'You takin' the bus out tonight?' he asked, wiping his oily hands on a bit of waste.

She managed to look fairly bright, and to say, 'Yes, please,' nicely, but it cost her a lot.

Duffy stood just inside the elevator, watching. The little runt bounced off into the darkness, and they heard him start up an engine. Duffy told himself that the engine was powerful all right. A minute later, the attendant brought round a big Cadillac, just with the parkers on. He brought the car round in a sweep, nailing it just where Annabel was standing. Duffy thought it was a nice piece of driving. It was.

The attendant dusted off the seat and held the door open for Annabel. Duffy might not have been there. He polished the wind-screen.

Annabel got in and slammed the door to. Duffy took hold of the trunk and looked at the attendant.

'Lend me some of your muscle,' he said.

The little runt was willing enough, but he was not much help. Duffy was sweating by the time they had fixed the trunk to the grid.

'She goin' away?' the attendant asked.

'Naw,' Duffy returned, testing the straps. 'Just getting rid of some books.'

'It's mighty late.'

Duffy looked at him sharply. Perhaps he wasn't so dumb as he looked. 'You mind?' he asked curtly.

The attendant blinked. He hastily said, 'I didn't mean anythin'.'

Duffy gave him a couple of bucks, then he went round the car and got in beside Annabel. She engaged the gear and the Cadillac rolled up the slipway.

'Where are we going?' she asked.

Duffy had already thought that one out. 'There's a little

burial ground on the East side, beyond Greenwich Village,' he said, 'we're going there.'

She shot a quick glance at him. 'That's cute,' she said.

Duffy leant back against the leather. 'You're a swell kid,' he said quietly, 'this is my unlucky day.'

She didn't say anything.

'I'll never bring this up again,' he said, 'but I can't leave it like that. I want you to know that I appreciate what you offered me, but that guy would have stiffened up by the time we were through, so I had to pass it up. You got plenty of reason to be sore at me.'

She said nothing for a few moments. 'I'm not sore at you,' she said at last. 'I think you're cute to throw me back at myself.'

Just like that. Duffy sighed and groped for a cigarette. 'Let's not fight,' he said, 'we've got enough on our hands.'

'I'm not fighting,' was all she said.

They rode the next three blocks in silence, then Duffy said, 'You turn right here.'

She swung the wheel. Duffy thought she handled the big Cadillac as if she were part of it. She judged distance to the closeness of the paint on her fender and the car threaded its way through the traffic without losing speed at any time. By uncanny anticipation she beat the lights most times. The Cadillac had plenty under the hood, and a touch on the pedal was enough to make it sweep forward like an arrow.

They came upon the burial ground as the clocks were striking two. Duffy leant forward. 'Take it easy,' he said, 'this is a lonely burg, but someone may be here.'

She stopped the car by the iron gates. Duffy opened the off door and got out. There were no lights to be seen in the burial ground; it was a pretty dark night.

Duffy was glad he wasn't Irish. The place was creepy. He turned to the car. 'You wait here,' he said. 'I'm just going to take a look round.'

She opened the door and stepped into the road. 'I'm not staying here alone,' she said.

Duffy wasn't surprised. He walked to the iron gates and pushed, they yielded, and swung open.

'Suppose you back the bus in,' he suggested, 'then we'll be off the road.'

She got in the Cadillac again and started the engine. Duffy let her run the car well down the centre lane of the graveyard and then signalled her to stop. He closed the iron gates again.

When she got out of the car, she was holding a small flashlight. The night air was close, and Duffy hooked a finger in his collar and jerked at it. He looked round the dim place. He didn't like it at all. She stood quite close to him, and he felt her shivering when he touched her.

Up above, the moon hung like a dead face, just visible through the mist. Duffy thought it was likely to rain any time.

'I want to find an old mausoleum,' he said. 'If we can park Cattley in one of them, he ain't likely to be turned up for some time, if ever.'

He began to walk slowly down the lane. Annabel kept close beside him. The white stones on each side of them looked ghostly. 'What a spot to be in,' Duffy thought.

As they penetrated further into the burial ground it got darker. The trees overhead began to get more dense.

'Nice spot this, ain't it?' Duffy said.

The heavy scent of graveyard flowers hung in the air. Underfoot, the cinders crunched, and sounded to Duffy like firecrackers.

'I wish we could get away from here,' Annabel said nervously, 'this scares me.'

'Me, I'm quaking,' Duffy said. 'I guess we're far enough off the road to chance having a little light.'

He swung the beam of the flash-light. It lit upon the tombstones, making them look startlingly white in the darkness.

'I think this looks like it.' Duffy paused and pointed the beam.

Over on the left stood a mausoleum in black marble. It was almost invisible until the beam showed it up. They went over and examined it carefully. The marble door was locked.

'This is Cattley's new home,' Duffy said, running his hand down the smooth cold door. 'But how the hell do we get him in?'

He put his shoulder against the door and heaved. He made his shoulder sore, but the door remained solid.

'What's that number there?' Annabel asked. She was holding the flash so that he could push against the door.

Duffy followed her eye. There was a small plate let in on the side of the door with a number 7 printed on it. Duffy said he didn't know.

'Do you think they keep the keys of these places at the porter's place?' she asked.

Duffy grinned at her. 'That's a grand idea,' he said. 'Let's go an' see.'

The porter's lodge, by the gates, was locked and deserted, but Duffy got a window open without much difficulty and looked round. He found a rack of keys by the front door, each key had a wooden tab hanging from it, with a number burnt into the wood. He looked for number 7 and found it.

'I believe you've got something,' he said. 'Suppose you drive the car up to the crypt while I go on and test the key.'

She got into the Cadillac and began to back it down the lane. He had to come back and help her with the flash, as she ran off the lane once or twice. They got back to the mausoleum at last and Duffy tried the key. The lock turned all right with some heavy pressure from Duffy, and he forced the door back. The air was bad down there, and he stepped away from the open door.

'That guy's going to have good company,' was all he said.

He went to the back of the car and wrestled with the straps that held the trunk. Annabel stood, holding the flash steady. He got the straps off and then levered the trunk to the ground. It was heavy, but he managed to get it down without making any noise. Then he stood up and wiped off his palms with his handkerchief.

'I guess I could do with a drink,' he said heavily.

'There's a pint flask in the driving-pocket.'

Duffy slipped round to the door pretty quick. He belted that pint hard. He thought it would be safer not to give Annabel any of it. Whisky seemed to take her in the wrong way. He didn't like to think of turning her down again.

'I guess I can tackle anything now,' he said, putting the flask in his hip pocket.

He took off his coat and undid his collar, pulling his tie loose. Then he walked over to the trunk and dragged it into the mausoleum. Annabel stood just outside the door, shining the flash. The beam jerked about. Her hand was shaking like a barman at work.

Duffy got the trunk inside and then paused.

'For God's sake gimme that light,' he said.

She seemed glad to do so. 'I'm going to be sick,' she said.

'No you ain't,' he said sharply. 'Go and sit in the car quick.'

When she had gone he opened the trunk and turned it on its side. The mackintosh parcel was jammed tight and he had to pull at it. The sheet suddenly tore in his hand and he went over backwards. He landed against a shelf, and his hand touched a cold metal strip. He fingered it, then he snatched his hand away. It was a handle of a coffin. His face oozed water as if it had been squeezed.

He went to the door and took a deep breath of the dank air, then he went back to the trunk. Savagely he pulled Cattley out, pulled away the cord, and jerked off the mackintosh sheet. Cattley sprawled at his feet. He didn't look at him. Dumping the sheet into the trunk, he pulled the trunk out of the crypt.

The whisky was hitting him all ends up now, and he lurched as he walked. He went back to get the flash, but he still didn't look at Cattley. Then he pulled the door of the mausoleum shut and shot the lock.

His shirt was sticking to his chest, and his legs were a little wobbly. Annabel called from the car, 'Are you all right?'

Duffy said he was fine, but that was because he was drunk. He didn't feel so good. He'd have liked to get so drunk right now that the whole of the evening could be washed out in sleep. He had had enough of it for one night.

She came out of the car and stood near him.

'What about the trunk?' she asked.

'Back at the lodge, there's a tap and hose for filling cans. I noticed it when I went in. I'll take these things over and wash 'em up, then we can go home.'

She sat on the running-board of the car and smoked a cigarette. She sat there the whole time with her eyes tight shut. She was so scared of being alone, that if it hadn't been for the cigarette between her lips she would have screamed and screamed.

On his way back, Duffy called to her when he was some distance away. He didn't want to come on her suddenly.

'It's okay,' he said, hoisting the trunk on to the grid again. 'There ain't no mess now. Cattley's planted good, so I guess that lets you out.'

She got into the Cadillac and drove slowly down to the gates. He walked beside the car. Opening the gates, he looked cautiously up and down the road, but it was dark and deserted. He shut the gates when she had driven into the road and climbed in beside her.

She drove at a furious pace without a word. Her eyes were fixed on the road ahead, and Duffy leant back, breathing heavily, his eyes heavy with sleep.

When they began to run into traffic again he raised his head. 'You can drop me off here,' he said. 'I'm going home.'

'I'll drive you there,' she said.

'No.'

She stopped the car.

'I'm sorry I . . .' she began.

'I'm going home,' Duffy said firmly. He had had a bellyful. 'Tomorrow, perhaps. Tonight, no.'

He opened the door and lurched on to the street. He stood there, holding the door in his hand. 'I've got to get those pictures back,' he said. 'I'll see you then.'

He slammed the door hard. He had a swift vision of her great eyes, wide with hate, her white teeth gleaming in the dark, then the Cadillac shot away from him.

He looked up and down the street for a taxi.

'I guess that honey hates my guts,' he said sadly, as a yellow taxi slid up to him.

CHAPTER FOUR

Duffy's place was a three-room affair on the top storey of an old-fashioned apartment house.

The taxi-driver drew up at the kerb, just under the street light. Duffy got out of the cab, letting the door swing on its hinges.

'This it?' the taxi-driver asked.

'Yeah, that's right.'

The taxi-driver looked at him. 'You been havin' a good time?'

Duffy shifted his head a little so that he didn't breathe over the taxi-driver.

He said, 'You don't know the half of it.'

The taxi-driver said, 'The first half's good enough for me.' One of those smart guys.

Duffy paid him off and slammed the door for him. He slammed the door so hard that the cab rocked. The taxi-driver scowled, but said nothing. He was smart all right, but he wasn't dumb. He rolled the cab away.

Duffy walked up the steps, fumbled for his key and fumbled at the lock. 'Jeeze, that Scotch was dynamite,' he said, as he poked at the lock. The key sank suddenly, and he turned it. The hall was in darkness, but he knew his way up. He started to climb the stairs as the wall-clock struck four. The wall-clock hung in the hall. It had a little brittle chime that always irritated Duffy. Treading carefully, one hand on the rail and the other just touching the opposite wall, he went up silently. He had to go up four flights, but he was used to that. When he reached his landing he paused. A light was burning in his apartment. He could see the bright light coming from under the door.

Two things crossed his mind. First, the cleaner had forgotten to turn the light off; and second, McGuire was waiting for him. It gave him quite a shock when he remembered McGuire. He had forgotten all about the poor guy. Too bad. He wagged his head. Maybe he'd be as sore as hell. He fumbled for his key again, and opened the door. The light quite blinded him for a second.

Two men were sitting in his room, facing the door. Another one was standing by the window, looking into the street, peeping round the blind.

Duffy jumped.

'I bet you've been stealing my whisky,' he said.

The man who was looking out of the window turned his head quickly. He was big. He had Mongolian eyes and a loose mouth. He had that battered, brutal face of an unsuccessful prize-fighter.

Duffy looked at him, then he looked at the two sitting in the chairs. The nearest one was a little guy with tight lips and cold, hard eyes. His face was white as cold mutton fat, and he just sat, with his hands folded across his stomach.

The other one, sitting on the little guy's right, was young. He had down on his cheeks and his skin had that peculiar rosy tint that most girls want, but don't have. He looked tough, because he had screwed up his eyes and drawn down the corners of his mouth. Duffy thought he was just movie-tough.

The little guy said, 'He's here at last.'

Duffy shut the door and leant against it. 'If I'd known you were coming,' he said, 'I'd been here sooner.'

The little guy said, 'Did you hear that? The bright boy said if he'd known we were coming, he'd been here sooner.'

The other two said nothing.

Duffy said, 'Now you're here, what's it all about?'

'He wants to know what's it all about,' the little guy said again.

Duffy slowly closed his fists. 'Must you repeat everything I say?' he asked. 'Can't these two birds understand what I say?'

The little guy eased himself back in his chair. 'You understand him, don't you, Clive?' he said to the youth.

'Clive?' Duffy was getting annoyed. 'That's the name for a daffodil, ain't it?'

The youth sat up. 'Listen, you long stick of—'

The little guy giggled. 'How do you think of such things?' he said.

'What *is* this?' Duffy demanded. He looked across at the tough bird by the window.

'Come on, come on,' the little guy said, suddenly looking bleak again. 'Give it up.'

'Give what up, for God's sake?' Duffy demanded.

'Did you hear him, Clive, he wants to know what to give up?'

The youth called Clive slouched out of his chair. He stood over the little guy, his face viciously angry. 'You won't get anywhere with this stuff,' he said. 'Turn Joe loose on him.'

The big bird on the corner took a step forward. He seemed to be holding himself in with difficulty. The little guy waved his hand at him. 'Not so fast,' he said, 'we ain't *got* to get rough with this lug.'

Duffy thought they were all screwy, and he wished he hadn't socked that pint away. Clive stood away from the little guy and glared at Duffy.

The little guy looked at Duffy with stony eyes. 'Get wise, bright boy,' he said. 'We've come for the camera.'

Duffy pushed his hat to the back of his head and blew out his cheeks. So that was it, he thought. He wandered over to the wagon and picked up a bottle of Scotch. 'You gentlemen want any of this?' he asked.

Clive had a gun in his hand. Duffy looked at it surprised, then he said to the little guy, 'Tell that fairy to put his rod away, he might hurt someone.'

The little guy said, 'I should care. What's it to me?'

Duffy said very sharply, 'Tell that punk to put his pop-gun down, or I'll do it for him, and smack his ears down.'

Clive made a high whinny sound like a horse. He looked as though he was going to have some sort of a fit. He stood there, his face white, and his eyes dark with hate. Duffy went a little cold at the sight of him.

The little guy said, 'Put it away.'

The youth turned his head slowly and looked at the little guy. 'I'm going to pop him ...' he said shrilly, all his words tumbling out of his mouth in a bunch.

'I said, put it away.' The little guy was quite shocked that he had to speak twice.

Clive hesitated, blinked, then pushed the gun into his hip pocket. He stood undecided, his hands fluttering at his coat. Then quite suddenly, he began to cry. His face puckered up like a little indiarubber mask that someone had squeezed. He sat himself on a chair and covered his face with his thin bony hands and cried.

The little guy sighed. He said to Duffy, 'See, you've upset him now.'

Duffy threw his hat on the settee and ran his fingers through his hair.

The big tough came over from the window and patted Clive's head. He didn't say anything, but just patted the youth quite heavily on his head.

The little guy shifted uncomfortably. 'Aw, I didn't mean anything,' he said. 'We ain't supposed to pop this guy, so I couldn't let you do it, could I?'

Clive took his hands away and said with a snivel, 'But look how you spoke to me.'

'Sure, sure, I know,' the little guy smiled with his tight mouth. 'I'm sorry. There, I can't say more, can I? I've said I'm sorry, that's pretty generous.'

Clive looked at the little guy earnestly. 'It wasn't what you said that upset me,' he said, 'it was how you said it.'

'I know, it was the way I said it, wasn't it?'

Clive began to cry again. He didn't cover his face this time, but screwed up his eyes, and wiped his nose with the back of his hand. 'Yes,' he said, 'it was the way you said it.'

'Quite a big shot, ain't he?' Duffy said, leaning against the wall, watching with extraordinary interest.

'You leave him alone,' the little guy said. 'He's all right, but he upsets himself.'

Clive stopped crying and shot Duffy a look of hate. The other two followed his glance, as if just remembering Duffy.

The little guy said to Clive, 'You all right now?'

Clive said he was fine.

'Come on,' the little guy said to Duffy, 'we're wasting time.'

Duffy said, 'I'm disappointed. I thought we were all going to let down our hair and have a good cry.'

The little guy giggled, then stopped and looked annoyed. 'Let's have the camera, we got to blow soon.'

Duffy lit a cigarette and blew a cloud of smoke to the ceiling. 'I ain't got it,' he said.

The three stayed very still.

'Listen,' the little guy said patiently, 'we've come for the camera, and we're going to have it, see?'

Duffy shrugged. 'I can't help that,' he said shortly, 'I ain't got it.'

The little guy said, 'You ain't got this right. I said we want that camera and we are going to have it.'

'Sure, I heard you the first time. I tell you I ain't got it.'

The little guy said, 'You ain't got this right. I said we want it.'

The youth drew his top lip off his teeth. 'I told you you weren't getting anywhere with this bastard.'

Duffy pushed himself away from the wall. He began to wander slowly round the room. He didn't take his eyes off the three, watching him.

'You be careful,' he said to Clive, 'you'll be getting some false teeth mighty soon.'

Clive looked at the little guy. 'Turn Joe on him,' he said excitedly. 'Go on, beat the sonofabitch to hell.'

Duffy was quite close to him now. He seemed to be carelessly looking for something. 'Don't call me that,' he said viciously, and his right fist came up from his waist slap in Clive's mouth. Duffy was nervous of the big bird. He thought with the other two out of the way, he might stand a chance with him, but he wasn't sure.

Clive went over, taking the chair with him. He lay on his side, hissing through his hand, that he had clapped to his mouth.

The other two were too startled to move. Duffy hit the little guy on the bridge of his nose. It was an awkward punch because the little guy was sitting but it had plenty of steam behind it. The little guy tossed back in his chair and went over with a crash. He lay there completely stunned.

Duffy stood, his hands a little advanced, his elbows pressed into his waist.

The big bird looked at Clive and then he looked at the little guy. Then he grinned, showing very white even little teeth. 'Jeeze!' he said hoarsely, 'you're going to get it now.'

He came in, weaving and bobbing. Duffy saw at once that he was right out of this fellow's class. He jumped away, and retreated until his heel thudded against the wall. The big bird came flat-footed but sure. His head was down, with his chin well tucked into his shoulder. Duffy let one go. It was a good one, coming up with a whistling sound. The big bird shifted a little, not much, but just a little, and Duffy's first hit the air. Then the big bird hit Duffy under the heart. It sounded like a cleaver going into a side of beef. Duffy thought the house had fallen on him. He felt his knees sag and the big bird let him come into a clinch. Duffy wound his arms round him, holding him so he couldn't hit him.

The big bird let him recover. He said, 'That was a good smack, huh?'

Duffy broke from the clinch, stepped back quickly, collided with a small table and went over backwards. He scrambled to his feet, hurriedly. The big bird gave him plenty of time, then he came in with that flat-footed shuffle, slipped Duffy's punch and banged Duffy in the ribs again. That punch hurt like hell. Again Duffy sagged at the knees; this time the big bird swung one to the side of his head and Duffy went over on his side and lay there. He landed quite close to the little guy, who was just sitting up. The little guy took a gun from inside his coat, holding it by the barrel, he leant forward and hit Duffy in the groin, hitting very hard.

Duffy curled into a ball, but he didn't yell. He bit his lip right through, but he didn't yell. Then he felt his inside coming up into his throat and he vomited.

The little guy shifted hastily. 'Look,' he said, 'the bastard nearly had me.' He got quite excited about it.

Clive said with approval, 'Now you're doing something.'

They stood round Duffy, watching him. The little guy pressing the bridge of his nose tenderly with his fingers, his eyes watering. Clive knelt on the floor with his lips swelling. He could feel that his front teeth moved a little when he touched them with his tongue. Joe stood with his hands hanging loose, like a dog deprived of its bone.

Duffy raised his head slowly. His face glistened with sweat. The shaded light from the ceiling lit his greenish skin. He was feeling awfully bad, but he held on to himself low down and rode with the pain. The blood ran down his chin from his lip. He could feel the salty taste in his mouth.

The little guy said, 'Give.'

Duffy didn't say anything. He didn't trust his voice. He lay there, his eyes on the little guy, hating him.

The little guy said, 'Ain't you had enough?'

Duffy still said nothing.

The little guy raised his hand. 'Soften him a little,' he said to Joe.

Joe smiled. He really took a pleasure in being tough. He put out an arm and his hand closed on Duffy's shirt front, then he heaved a little. Duffy came up, like a cork out of a bottle. He gave a little grunt of anguish. His open hand smacked Joe across the eyes. Joe blinked. 'Did you see what he did to me?' he said.

The little guy said, 'Full of fight, ain't he?'

Duffy swung at Joe feebly, his punch wouldn't have knocked down a child. Joe grinned. 'Get wise to yourself, bright boy,' he said. 'You ain't hurting no one.'

The little guy said, 'Just pat him around a bit, will you, Joe? We ain't got much time.'

Joe said, 'Sure.' He held Duffy at arm's length and hit him between the eyes. His fist travelled at a tremendous speed. Duffy could see it coming, but he couldn't avoid it. Something exploded in his brain, and a bright flash of brightness blinded him. He wanted to lie down, but something was holding on to him.

The little guy said, 'Now don't hit him too hard, just pat him around.' His voice sounded a long way away to Duffy.

'I know just what you want,' the big bird said, and he started to slap Duffy's face with heavy resounding blows with his open hand.

The little guy said to Clive, 'If this makes you feel bad, you can turn your head.'

Clive said, 'I'm feeling fine. I wish I was as big as Joe.'

The little guy patted his arm. 'I don't,' he said.

When Joe got tired, he said; 'Shall we try him now?'

The little guy said, 'I think so.'

Joe let go of Duffy, who fell in a heap on the floor. His face was a sight. The little guy knelt down. 'Where's the camera, bright boy?'

Duffy mumbled something, but his mouth was so swollen that the little guy couldn't hear what he said.

'Lay him up on the couch, Joe, we'll have to get him into shape.'

Joe pulled Duffy across the floor by his arm and dumped him on to the over-stuffed couch.

'Get some water, Clive, and a towel,' the little guy said.

Clive went out of the room into the bathroom. Duffy lay with his eyes shut, his breath coming in shuddering gasps.

Joe went over to the wagon and poured himself out a drink. He took it neat, then punched himself on the chest with his fist.

Clive came back with a wet towel. The little guy held out his hand, but Clive walked over to Duffy. 'Let me do it.'

'Well, well, did you hear, Joe?' the little guy was surprised. 'Clive wants to do it.'

Clive went on one knee beside Duffy and mopped his swollen bruised face with the towel. Duffy looked at him through a puffy eye. Then Clive put his hand on the side of Duffy's head, made his fingers into claws and dragged his nails down Duffy's face.

The little guy ran across the room and pulled Clive away. Clive had flecks of foam at the sides of his mouth. 'That'll teach him,' he said shrilly. 'He won't hit me again in a hurry.'

'You might have broken your nice nails,' the little guy said sharply. 'That ain't the way to go on.'

Duffy pushed himself up on the couch and lowered his legs to the floor. Joe watched him, a big grin on his face. 'Ain't he a pip?' he said, admiringly.

The other two turned and watched him too. Duffy was sitting up now, his head sunk on his chest. He remained like that for several minutes, then he put both hands on the couch and levered himself to his feet. His face was a mask of blood. Swaying, he made a little tottering run at Clive, who hastily got behind the little guy.

Joe stepped in front of Duffy. He said, 'Still looking for trouble?'

Duffy swung a leaden arm, but Joe hit him in the ribs again, stepping in close and driving at Duffy a jarring jolt. Duffy opened his mouth and said 'O!', then he fell on his knees.

Just then the telephone bell rang. The three started and looked at the telephone. It continued to ring.

'That's bad,' the little guy said, looking worried.

They waited, all concentrated on the sound of the bell. It rang for several seconds, then it stopped.

Joe dragged Duffy on to the couch again. He heaved him up and looked at the little guy.

'Bring him round,' the little guy said.

Joe pulled Duffy's ears. He took them in each hand and tugged as if he were milking a cow. Duffy groaned and tried to get his head away.

'He's here now,' Joe said.

The little guy stood quite close to Duffy. 'Come on,' he said loudly, 'spill it. Where's that goddam camera?'

'Somebody stole it,' Duffy mumbled only half conscious.

The little guy stood back. 'Christ!' he said. 'Did you hear that? He said someone stole it. This bird must be nuts to hang on so long.'

The telephone bell began to ring again. Clive said suddenly, 'Perhaps it's Mr. Morgan.'

The little guy said, 'Quiet,' and looked at Duffy. Duffy lay with his eyes shut, but he had heard all right. His brain wouldn't think, but he remembered all right. The little guy hesitated, then went over to the 'phone. He unhooked the receiver from its prong.

'Hellow?' he said in his tight voice.

He stood listening. Then he said, 'You got a wrong number, buddy,' and hung up. He shook his head. 'Some guy wanting this bird,' he jerked his thumb at Duffy. 'Suppose you try him again, Joe?'

Clive took a step forward. 'Why don't you burn him a little?' he demanded. 'This is wasting time.'

The little guy looked at Joe. 'Do you think you can shake him loose?' he said.

Joe grinned. 'Yeah,' he said; 'give me a little time. This pip thinks I am playing with him, don't you, bright boy.'

Duffy was getting light-headed, but he felt a little strength stealing into his legs. 'Wait a minute,' he said with difficulty. 'Can't you believe what I tell you? Some bird stole that camera before I left the dame's house. I've just come back. I ain't got it on me, have I?'

The little guy put his hand on Joe's arm.

'Maybe he's telling it straight,' he said.

Joe shook his head. 'That guy couldn't tell it straight to a priest,' he said.

The little guy looked at the clock on the mantelshelf. 'Look at the time,' he said.

Clive said, 'It's all talk ... talk ... talk ... talk!'

The little guy patted him on his arm. 'If he ain't got the camera, what can I do?'

Duffy sat up slowly and passed a hand over his face gently. Near by, on the arm of the couch, was an ash-tray. One of those affairs with a leather spring that gripped the arm. It was quite a heavy thing. Duffy put his hand on it, then with one movement, he picked it off the arm of the couch and tossed it through the window. The glass shattered, making a high tinkling sound. Some of the glass fell in the street below.

The little guy said, 'Clever, ain't he?'

Clive ran to the door. 'Let's skip before the cops come up,' he said.

The little guy said, 'Sure we'll go.' Then he looked at Duffy. 'We'll be back, bright boy.'

He followed Clive out of the room.

Joe clouted Duffy on the side of the head. The blow knocked him off the couch on to the floor. 'We'll get together by'n by,' he said, and went to the door hurriedly, then he paused, looking at Duffy lying there. He came back and kicked Duffy very hard in the ribs.

The little guy put his head round the door.

'Come on, Joe,' he said, 'we gotta get out of this.'

Joe followed him from the room, shutting the door quietly behind him.

Duffy lay on the floor, his knees drawn up to his chin. After they had been gone some time, he began to sob a little.

CHAPTER FIVE

A voice said, 'What a guy!'

Duffy forced one swollen eyelid back and tried to see who it was. A blurred figure was standing over him. He thought it might be Joe again, so he shut his eye and lay still.

'Bill!'

That wasn't Joe, he thought; it sounded like McGuire. Duffy raised his head painfully. 'I think you've come a little late,' he said with a faint groan.

McGuire said, 'My Gawd!' and meant it. 'What the hell have you been doing with yourself?'

Duffy turned a little to the wall. He wasn't quite ready for any bright talk. 'Gimme a break,' he said faintly.

McGuire was so upset and astonished, he just stood gaping at Duffy. Then he looked round the room, seeing the over-turned furniture, the mess of the blood, and the blood-smears on the wall. 'What's been going on round here? Jeeze! This looks as if a massacre came off not so long ago.'

Duffy said through his clenched teeth, 'ME, I'm it.'

McGuire took another look at him, then hurried into the bathroom. He found a small bowl and a towel. He filled the bowl with tepid water, and came back to Duffy again.

'Come on, soldier,' he said. 'Let's make you look a bit ship-shape.'

'Suppose you go take a pill,' Duffy said with difficulty.

'Now come on.' McGuire put the bowl on the floor and dropped the towel into the water. He squeezed the towel and began wiping Duffy's face with awkward care. He was as tender as a woman to Duffy.

Duffy said suddenly, 'Hi, you rat, be careful of my nose.'

McGuire said, 'You don't call that a nose any more, do you?'

When he cleared the dried blood away, he took the bowl into the bathroom and changed the water. Deep down, a burning anger smouldered against those who had done this to Duffy. McGuire was one of those guys who made few friends, but when he had picked one, he stuck. He was, on the surface, casual and a great kidder, but he'd stick like a burr and fight once he had found a friend. Duffy and he had knocked along together on the *Tribune* for some little while. They had quarrelled, kidded, and double-crossed each other, but let anyone else start anything then they'd side up together and beat hell out of the intruder.

He filled the bowl with water again and walked back to Duffy.

'For God's sake, you must be losing your grip or something,' Duffy mumbled from the couch.

'What now?'

'Listen, dimwit, instead of pulling this Flo Nightingale act, what the hell's wrong in giving me a drink?'

McGuire put the bowl down on the table. 'You're right,' he said. 'This business startled me.' He went over to the wagon and poured out two stiff Scotches. He was going to hold the glass to Duffy's mouth, but Duffy took the glass from him roughly. 'For the love of Mike,' Duffy said, 'don't you think I can help myself to Scotch?'

They both felt better after the drink. McGuire said, 'Was that some woman you brought home who set about you like that?'

Duffy put his glass on the floor and sat up very slowly. He put his hands over his groin and his mouth twisted. McGuire watched him uneasily. 'You all right?'

'Sure, I'm all right,' Duffy said. 'I'm fine.'

'All right, tough guy, but you can take it easy for a moment. Here, lie back, will you?'

Duffy swung his feet over the side of the couch, then he stood up. As soon as his legs had to take his weight, he bent in half. He would have fallen forward if McGuire hadn't taken his arm.

'I'm getting soft, I guess,' Duffy said, sweat starting out on his face.

McGuire led him back to the couch and sat him down.

'Quit this stuff,' he said impatiently. 'Lie down, or I'll smack your ears for you.'

Duffy sank back on the couch. He was glad to.

McGuire poured him out another Scotch, and after that he felt his strength coming back.

'Suppose you tell me what happened?'

'Sure. I ran into three toughs who pushed me around.'

McGuire shook his head. 'Do you want me to call in the cops?'

'This ain't for the cops.'

'Okay, what now?'

'What's the time?'

'It's getting on for ten o'clock.'

Duffy groaned. 'What a hell of a night I had,' he said, resting his head on his hands.

McGuire went over to the telephone and dialled a number. Duffy watched him curiously. He heard the line connect with a little plop, then McGuire said, 'Sam here, honey.' Then, after a pause he went on. 'This crazy loon's got himself into a jam. You ought to see him. Gee! He looks terrible. Yeah, someone pushed him around. Well, I don't think he's capable of taking care of himself, so I'm bringing him right round to you. Fix up the spare bed for him, will you?' He stood listening for quite a while, then he said, 'Coming right now,' and he hung up.

Duffy said heatedly, 'If you think you're going to turn that wife of yours loose on me—'

'Pipe down,' McGuire said sharply 'you're doing what you're told. Listen, you small-time prizefighter, you come on your feet or you come on your ear, it's all the same to me.'

'Okay, I'll come.'

McGuire had quite a job getting him over to his place, but he did it. The taxi-driver who brought them took an extraordinary interest in Duffy. He helped McGuire get him out of the cab and up the steps. Then he stood there, shaking his head.

McGuire got a little heated about it. 'All right, all right,' he said; 'ain't you seen someone pushed around before?'

'He ain't been pushed around,' the taxi-driver said, looking Duffy over, 'someone's been making love to him.'

McGuire shut the door in his face.

On the third floor Alice was waiting for them in the passage. A tall, dark girl, with black hair dressed low that set off her olive complexion, and gave her just a slight foreign look. Her large eyes, alight with life, were now large and scared.

It didn't matter how low Duffy felt, Alice always made him feel good. When she saw him, she put her hand quickly to her mouth. Her skin went a little paler, so that it looked almost oyster colour in the sunlit corridor. Her eyes filled with tears, but that was as far as she would show her feelings.

'Bill Duffy!' she said, 'how could you?'

McGuire said, 'A real fighting drunk, ain't he?'

Duffy tried a grin, but it was so painful to him and to look at, he hastily took it off his face. 'This ain't anything,' he kidded; 'you ought to've seen me when I put Dempsey to sleep.'

'He's light-headed,' Alice said, but she put her hand on his arm. 'Get him inside quickly, Sam.'

McGuire said, 'I'll be glad to. The way he's leaning on me, you'd think he's hurt.'

They took him into McGuire's little flat. A pleasant four-room box of a place, bright and comfortable. Everywhere, Alice had left something of herself. The neatness, the sweet-smelling flowers, the shine of the stained boards, showed the woman's hand. Duffy looked round the sitting-room regretfully. Whenever he saw it, he felt a faint hunger. He had never made a secret about it. If McGuire hadn't married Alice, he would have. The three of them were close linked.

When McGuire got him undressed and into the cool sheets, he relaxed, and the pain that was riding his body gradually began to ease. Alice came in a moment later, fixed his pillow, fussed round him with a scent bottle, and Duffy loved it.

McGuire looked at his watch. 'Let the animal sleep,' he said to Alice. 'I gotta go and work. Keep away from him. If he gets fresh, call a cop.' Then looking at Duffy, he said, 'Take a nap, soldier, I'll have a little chin with you later.'

Duffy said, 'I'll steal your wife from you.'

Alice and Sam exchanged glances, Duffy watched them through his swollen eyes. He thought they looked a swell pair. He shut his eyes for a moment, then found it was too much trouble to open them again.

Alice looked down at him. 'What can have happened to the poor dear?' she said, keeping her voice very low.

McGuire put his arm round her and they left the room together. 'He said three toughs set about him,' he said, when they were in the living-room. 'Let him have a good sleep, then we'll hear something more. I'll get back early tonight.'

'Sam!' Duffy's voice was urgent.

McGuire went back into the bedroom. 'Go to sleep, you big loon,' he commanded.

'Listen, Sam.' Duffy raised his head. 'I want you to find out all you can about a girl called Annabel English, a guy called Daniel Morgan and whoever works for him. Dig in and get the lowdown on them. Don't miss a thing. Also find out what you can about Cattley the dope-peddler. Get that, and I'll rest all right.'

McGuire took out a note-book and jotted down the names. 'All right,' he said; 'it all sounds screwy to me, and I'm bursting with curiosity, but I'll get you the dope, but in the meantime, take it easy.'

When McGuire got back in the evening, Duffy was still sleeping.

Alice said, 'He's been that way all day.'

'Sure, that's the best thing that could happen to him. Suppose we eat, and then maybe he'll be ready to talk.'

While Alice was serving up, Duffy woke. He got into a dressing-gown and came out into the sitting-room. He looked a lot worse than he felt.

Alice said, 'Bill Duffy, go straight back to bed!'

'I wish you two wouldn't pick on me,' Duffy said, sitting in an easy chair, 'I'm feeling good. Hi, Sam, what about a drink?'

The other two looked at each other helplessly.

'A hopeless soak,' Sam said sadly. 'You better go back.'

Duffy shook his head. 'You two birds had better be careful,' he said, 'I've just had a little fast training, and I'll get tough.'

McGuire settled the argument by producing a bottle of rum, a squeezer, some fresh limes, and a bottle of absinthe. He set about making up some Bacardi Crustas.

'Make 'em big and strong,' Duffy said, 'I want to get cock-eyed tonight.'

Alice looked round the kitchen door. 'I've been waiting for that all day,' she said.

'My wife's an awful drunkard,' Sam said.

'You're telling me?' Duffy stood up to look at himself in the mirror. He took one glance, grimaced and sat down again. 'I remember, before you knew her, when she got so stewed that it took ten cops to handle her.'

Sam poured out the drinks. 'That's old stuff,' he said, 'you don't know what she's like now. Give her a few shots of rum, and it takes an army to handle her.'

Alice came in. 'When you two loafers've finished pulling my reputation to bits, come on in and eat.'

They followed her into the kitchen, Duffy walking slowly, careful not to touch anything, and Sam with the big shaker in his hands.

They sat round the table. Duffy found it was difficult to eat, but he made a good show. They talked about general things until the meal was over. Both Alice and Sam were burning with curiosity, but they let Duffy have his head. When they had finished, they went back into the sitting-room. Alice sat herself on the arm of Duffy's chair, and McGuire stood in front of the empty fire-grate.

Duffy said, 'I'm sorry to keep you waiting. I guess you'd better have it from the start, and then we'll go into the whys and whats after.'

He told them everything. How he met Morgan, what Morgan wanted him to do, how he went to the house and took the photographs, how the camera was stolen, how he found Cattley in the lift-shaft, how he got rid of the body, the meeting with the three toughs. He gave them the whole works.

When he had finished, there was a long silence. Then McGuire said, 'You've started something this time.'

'I've not only started something, but it's something I'm going to finish.'

Alice ran her long fingers through his hair. 'I know it's no good me saying anything, but don't you think you've done enough?'

Duffy put his fingers tenderly on his face, his eyes were suddenly very bleak. 'No one can push me around like this and not know something about it,' he said softly.

Alice got off the arm of his chair and walked over to the fireplace. She stood looking down at Duffy, her big eyes were sad. 'You men are all alike,' she said; there was a faint undertone of bitterness in her voice. 'All tough guys, who come home hurt!'

Duffy looked over at Sam. 'Suppose we forget that for a moment,' he said; 'tell me what you found out about Annabel English.'

Sam began to fill a pipe. 'That dame's going to get herself into trouble one of these days,' he said, fumbling around for some matches. Alice took a box off the mantelshelf and gave them to him. 'One of these days, she's going to be stuck for a sucker, and then she'll be landed in the cooler.'

Duffy said, 'I want facts, not an extract from *True*.'

'Well, in brief, she's Edwin English's daughter. I supposed you guessed that?'

Duffy looked startled. 'No,' he said seriously, 'I should have thought of that, but I didn't.'

'Do you mean Edwin English, the politician?' Alice asked.

Sam nodded shortly. 'Yeah,' he said, 'Annabel's the wild one of the family. English stands for anti-vice, you know all about his racket. Annabel's his big thorn. I guess she about crucifies the old man. About three years ago they agreed to part. He set her up in a swell apartment, and gave her a big allowance, on condition that she behaved herself, and didn't give him any cause for getting in bad with his voters.'

Duffy said, 'I'd just hate to be an anti-vice candidate with a daughter like that.'

Sam nodded. 'You bet,' he said, 'this little dame's a nympho-something or other, I forget the word. You know, she's hot for anything in pants.'

'You mean nymphomaniac?' Alice said, 'isn't that rather strong?'

'Strong?' Duffy broke in. 'Say listen . . .' He paused, changed his mind, and went on, 'never mind. It ain't too strong. Go on, Sam.'

'The old man's for ever steaming himself in case she breaks out, and stains the family name. You know the type of thing. The other politicians are just praying that she does start something. They all hate English like hell. I don't wonder at it. That guy's mind is so narrow, he overbalances every time he uses it.'

'Anything more?'

Sam shrugged. 'A lot of hushed-up scandal that won't help you much,' he said. 'English has paid plenty during the last two years, keeping her out of gaol and out of the papers. She goes to every smut night-club in town. She's on the list for getting smut cine-films for private exhibition. She's had three or four fancy boys who've been mixed up in shady business. And so on. Not a nice little girl.'

Duffy brooded. 'Somehow,' he said, 'I guessed as much.'

'Now you know all this,' Alice said quietly, 'you are not going to do anything further?'

'You're a swell kid.' Duffy got up and went over to her. 'Quit worrying, can't you? I don't care how bad that dame is, I started this damn' business. I was sucker enough to take those photos, and I guess I'm getting them back.'

Alice sighed. 'Worthless women always seem to get help from men,' she said. 'I suppose it is so easy to fool a really fine man.'

Duffy exchanged glances with Sam. 'Skip it, Alice,' Sam said. 'You know what Bill is. You're holding us up.'

Alice forced a little smile. 'I'm sorry,' she said and sat down in Duffy's chair. Duffy came and sat on the arm.

'What about Morgan?'

Sam blew out a cloud of smoke. 'Now Morgan, he's a cagey bird to nail. He's got some racket in connection with a chain of night-clubs. I'd say at a guess, he's a boss behind the scene, and he's controlling vice in a big way. Anyway, I can't get a proper line on him, except rumours. They know him down at headquarters, but they've never pinned anything to him yet. Still, they're always hoping. He's got plenty of dough, runs a big house, and has a tough mob working for him.'

'If Morgan's got that sort of a background, I guess he'd want those pictures of that girl. It might give him enough pull to scare English off closing his joints.' Duffy was looking thoughtful.

Sam nodded. 'That's just it,' he said. 'Morgan would be sitting very pretty if he could close English down.'

'Cattley? Did you find out anything fresh about him?' Duffy asked.

Sam shrugged. 'There's not much you don't know about that rat,' he said, 'you know what he did. Dope, women, and white slaving. Cattley's certainly been making plenty of dough these last months. No one's sure of where he got it. He's moved up a lot since we knew him. Does, or rather did, everything on a big scale. The cops can't get a line on him, but they watch him from time to time.'

'Is he going to be missed?'

Sam shrugged. 'Not unless someone who knows him gets worried and blows to the police. That ain't likely.'

Duffy brooded some more. 'You done a swell job of work,' he said at last. 'What I want to know, is where do I go from here?'

Sam said, 'I'd take it easy for a bit.'

Duffy shook his head. 'I got to get those pictures,' he said, 'and I've got to 'em fast.'

Alice said, 'Has Morgan got them, do you think?'

'No. Morgan hasn't got them. It was Morgan's crowd who pushed me around. It looks to me that some other party has horned in and helped themselves. Just as long as Cattley remains in that vault, trouble will stay still. As soon as he pokes up his head, the balloon will go up.'

'Don't you run a risk of being made an accessary after the fact or something?' Alice asked, her brow wrinkled.

Duffy said, 'I guess I've been in worse spots than accessary charges.'

Sam got up and began to pile the plates in the kitchen. Alice went out to help him. Duffy sat in the arm-chair and brooded. His body was one dull ache, but he wouldn't let his mind dwell on it. There was a bitter angry feeling smouldering inside him. Furious with Morgan, revengeful against those three toughs, and determined to get those photos back, he thought of Annabel. Then he got up and went over to the telephone. He dialled a number, after consulting the book.

He recognized her voice at once.

'This is Duffy here,' he said.

'Have you got them?' her voice was eager.

'Listen, baby,' he said, speaking low and fast, 'you don't know half what happened last night.'

'What is it?'

'For one thing Morgan ain't got those pictures. For another, he wants them mighty bad. When I got home last night, three birds were waiting for me and they beat me silly when I couldn't give them the camera.'

She was silent for a moment. 'But who has got it?' she said at last.

'I don't know,' he had to admit it; 'this is a line up against your Pa. Why the hell didn't you tell me who you were?'

'Well, who am I?'

'You're Edwin English's daughter.'

'I prefer to say I am Annabel English.'

He laughed. He couldn't help himself. 'I've been looking up your record, baby, it ain't so hot.'

'You think so?' She sounded very cool. 'I thought you'd appreciate me.'

'I think you ought to go very slow for a bit,' he said, 'you just lie low, and don't start anything. It wouldn't be a bad idea for you to get out of town for a little while.'

'Oh no,' she was very definite, 'I won't do that.'

'Okay, but watch your step from now on.'

'When am I seeing you?'

He grinned, but he felt no mirth. 'Sooner than you think,' he said quietly, and hung up.

CHAPTER SIX

It took Duffy two impatient days to shake himself loose. Sam and Alice, their nerves frayed, were at last forced to give way to his insistence.

In a new suit, his face still battered, his temper vile, Duffy walked into the street. Sam came along at his heels.

'I feel,' said Sam, 'that you're going to run into trouble so fast we ain't going to have any time to stick you together again.'

Duffy was walking fast. 'You don't know nothing,' he said shortly; 'I feel fine, and I ain't going to find trouble.'

Sam swung along at his side. 'What's the hurry, for God's sake? You got a date with someone?'

'No, but I got to get me some exercise. Come on, get going.'

'You ain't said where you're going,' Sam said.

'First I'm going back to my joint, then I'm going to find out something about Cattley.'

'Why Cattley, for the love of Mike?'

'Just that; I don't know. Maybe, I've got a hunch. Cattley's at the bottom of this, and I want to find out quite a bit about him. I want to find out why he was rubbed out. When I find that out, I guess I'll be pretty close to his killer. Okay, when I find his killer, I'll find the camera.'

Sam stopped at the corner. 'Well, I can't run around with you all day. I've got a living to make. Now, soldier, you're coming back to us tonight, ain't you?'

'Listen, Sam, you're swell, and Alice's swell. You're both swell, but from now on, you keep out of this. I'm going my own little way, without you two popping your heads into anything I might stir up.'

Sam groaned. 'I love you like this; just a big selfish playboy. You have the fun and we're just to sit round to put on the adhesive tape. Listen, mug, we're both in this, get it?'

Duffy grinned. It still hurt him to grin, but he grinned. 'I'll be along,' he said, 'I get it.'

Sam looked pleased. 'Bounce 'em brother, bounce 'em,' he said.

'They'll take some bouncing,' Duffy said ruefully, as he watched McGuire's long frame disappearing through the crowded traffic.

He walked down the street, conscious of quick furtive glances at his battered face. He felt suddenly angry, his eyebrows coming down, making his face even more unattractive.

When he reached his apartment he was glad to find the place had been cleaned up. He made a little grimace at the faint stains on the walls. He wandered through the rooms, looking at everything carefully. Then he returned to the sitting-room. He sat on the edge of the table and thought a little while.

Cattley must have an apartment somewhere. The telephone directory gave him the information. He dialled the number opposite Cattley's name, but there was no answer.

Going down once more into the street, he flagged a taxi and gave an address on the East side. After he had gone a little way, he glanced out of the small rear window. A big Packard was rolling along behind him. He thought, 'Maybe I'm just jumpy,' but he watched the Packard closely. After he had been riding for several minutes he leant forward. 'A bird's sitting on our tail,' he said abruptly. 'It makes me nervous.'

The taxi-driver was a big beefy Irishman. He turned his head and grinned. 'Watch me shake 'em,' he said.

Duffy gave him five minutes, then said again. 'You'll have to do better than that.'

The driver pushed the cab until it began to rattle but the Packard just sat behind them.

Duffy said, 'He's too big for you.'

'What do you want me to do, boss?'

Duffy fumbled for some money. He gave the driver a couple of bucks. 'Drop me at the first boozer you see,' he said; 'don't stop, just slow down. If they come after you, you don't know where you were taking me.'

'Like the movies, huh?'

'Sure, you got it. Like the movies.'

The driver suddenly crowded on his brakes and swung to the kerb. Duffy bundled out, slamming the door. He stood on the pavement, watching the cab drive on. The Packard slowed down, hesitated, then shot away at right angles, turning a corner, disappearing quickly. Duffy didn't see who was in it. He flagged another cab and told the driver to drive on for a while. When he was sure that he hadn't got the Packard on his tail, he gave the apartment address again.

Cattley's apartment was big and showy. It was on the second floor of a large block. Duffy didn't take the elevator up, he walked. On the front door, was a small metal plate bearing Cattley's name. Duffy rang the bell. No one answered. He stood waiting. Then he rang the bell again. While he was standing there, he heard the elevator coming up. He stepped away from the door quickly and went up three stairs of the next flight. He was just out of sight from the elevator. He heard the grille slide back, and he looked round cautiously. A woman was standing in front of Cattley's door. He couldn't see who she was, but he watched her closely. There was something very familiar in her slim figure. She took a key from her handbag and opened the door. He came down the three stairs silently and walked into the room behind her.

'Hello, baby,' he said.

She stood quite still for a moment, then turned and faced him. Her face was a little drawn, and her eyes big.

'You frightened me.'

Duffy thought she had an iron nerve. 'Nice to see you again,' he said.

Annabel English looked at him. Then she put a hand quickly on his arm. 'But your face,' she said, 'what has happened?'

Duffy touched his face with his finger-tips, then smiled; it was a very bleak smile. 'I told you,' he said, 'some toughs pushed me around.'

'It's horrible.' She came closer to him. 'They must have hurt you so.'

Duffy shrugged. 'Forget it,' he said; 'what brings you up here?'

She turned from him and wandered away across the room to the window. It was a shabby room. Duffy was quite surprised.

The address was good enough, but Cattley had let the place run to seed. The furniture was old and battered and the walls needed attention. There was dust everywhere.

Duffy stood watching her. 'What brings you up here?' he repeated.

When she reached the window she turned, so that the light was behind her. 'I wanted to look round,' she said; 'why are you here?'

He lit a cigarette. 'You know, baby,' he said, moving further into the room and sitting on the corner of the table. 'I don't think we're going to get along so well together.'

'Oh, but yes.'

He shook his head. 'I guess I got you into a spot the other night, but you ain't doing anything to help me get you out of it. You're holding back on me.'

She came over to him. 'May I smoke?' she said.

He took out his case and she took one. He lit it for her. 'Your poor face,' she said softly.

'Quit stalling,' he said impatiently. 'You know, if you don't play ball, I'm going to ditch you.'

'Please don't get that way.' She went and sat down in a low, overstuffed chair. She crossed her legs, and Duffy grinned.

'You women,' he said, 'you think you've only got to show what you've got, and a man will roll over on his back, with his paws raised. Now, listen, this is important. What are you doing up here? How did you get a key to this joint?'

She studied her red finger-nails. 'Suppose I said that I can't tell you?'

'Okay, you can't tell me. Well, those photos can take care of themselves.'

She raised her heavy lashes and looked at him. 'Honest, Bill, just now I can't tell you.'

He slid off the table. 'I'm going to look round this joint,' he said shortly, 'you sit there.'

He went into the bedroom and began a systematic search. Patiently he went through every drawer, examined the sides of the arm-chair, looked behind the few pictures of doubtful taste hanging on the walls, took the grubby bed to pieces, but he found nothing to interest him. He went into the small kitchen and hunted about there. Then he stood still and scratched his head. He didn't know what he was looking for, but he had hoped that he would have found something to give him a lead. He went to the kitchen door. Then his eyes narrowed. Annabel was sitting quite still, but he knew that she had moved from the chair whilst he was in the kitchen. Her elaborate calmness, her frank smile when he came into the room, told him.

'Have you found anything?' she said, with a great show of interest.

He began wandering round the room. 'Not yet,' he said, 'but I'm getting hot.'

She got out of the chair. 'Where's the Johnny?'

He stood quite still, then he jerked his head.

'Just through the bedroom,' he said.

'I won't be a minute.'

He didn't say anything, but watched her go into the bedroom, then he heard her shoot the bolt on the bathroom door.

He saw that she had left her bag on the table, and he went over quickly and scooped it up. He pressed on the paste diamond clasp and opened it. Quickly he emptied the contents on the table. There was the usual collection of junk that most women carry. A powder compact, cigarette-case and lighter, a lipstick in a gold case, a small phial of scent, some letters, and a roll of greenbacks. Nothing to interest him.

Making a little grimace of annoyance, he pushed the stuff back into the bag.

Then he began to examine the room carefully. The drawers yielded nothing, but on the sideboard he noticed a cigarette box had been moved. He could see the outline of dust had been disturbed. He opened the box, but it was empty. He took it over to the window and examined it carefully. Putting his fingers inside, he gently pushed. The bottom of the box suddenly sprang up. There was nothing in the false bottom. He took the box back and put it on the sideboard again.

Annabel came into the room again, touching her red hair with her finger-tips. She was quite calm. He looked her over thoughtfully.

'Finished?' she asked, going over to the table and picking up her bag. 'Suppose you come and have some coffee with me?'

Duffy mashed his cigarette out in the tray. He held out his hand. 'Give,' he said.

She raised her eyebrows. 'Now don't start being silly,' she said, there was a faint note of anger in her voice.

Duffy walked over to her. 'Come on,' he said roughly. 'Hand it over.'

'What *is* this?' She turned impatiently to the door.

Duffy said evenly, 'Wait a minute, sister, you and I are going to have a little talk.'

She looked over her shoulder at him. Her eyes were stormy. 'We're going right out of this place,' she said. 'I'll talk to you over coffee.'

Duffy wandered over to the door and set his broad back against it. 'We'll talk right here,' he said briefly.

She shrugged and leant against the table. 'Well, what is it?'

'I want you to get this business straight,' he said; 'up to now you've been acting like a dimwit all along. Well, you gotta wake up to things. You and I are in a murder mix-up. You stand a sweet chance of getting fried, and I'm in line for an accessary rap. You're playing it like an afternoon tumble with the curtains drawn. Get wise to it, Redhead.'

She tapped on the floor with her shoe. 'I know all that,' she said, 'but that gets me nowhere.'

The smile on his face was hard. 'You're holding back on me, baby, and you know it,' he said. 'If I weren't in this as an accessary, I'd let it ride. I'm in this for two reasons. One, I'm in it, if you get pinched, and two, I've got a little score to settle with Morgan. I'm easy enough if you play ball, but I'll get goddam' hard if you don't.'

She said suddenly in a sharp voice, 'Let me out of here.'

Duffy didn't move. 'You're in a spot, sister,' he said, 'there is only one way you can get out of here. You can open your pretty mouth and start squawking, and that'll bring the cops arunnin', asking questions. You'll have a sweet twenty minutes, explaining why you're here, and how you got the key to this joint. Then they'll start looking for Cattley, and suppose they find him, what then?'

She looked at him thoughtfully, then a little smile broke on her lips. 'All right,' she said, 'if that's the way you feel, let's talk.'

Duffy shook his head sadly. 'My, my,' he said. 'You're like an eel, ain't you? Tough one minute, then the soft pedal. It ain't getting you anywhere, sister. You came here to find something and you've found it. Okay, you and me are going to share it.'

She swung herself on the table, so that her skirt rode above her knees. Duffy looked at them, and thought they were nice. 'You know everything,' she said; 'you're quite right, I did come here to find something. I suppose I'd better tell you all about it.'

Duffy grinned. 'And with perfect grace, she confessed the truth,' he said.

'Well, I've been a fool,' she said, studying her nails; 'naturally, I wanted to keep it to myself. You've guessed by now that I lied to you about writing a book?'

Duffy said, 'You'd be surprised how much I do know.'

'Cattley was blackmailing me,' her voice was suddenly weary; 'I've had to pay and pay. I did something crazy once and Cattley was there. My father would have been in a hopeless position to run for election if it got out, and Cattley was smart enough to know this. He put the screws on, and I had to pay. It's awful of me to say this, but his death was a great relief to me.'

Duffy said, 'You're giving me a grand motive for his killing.'

She slid off the table and came over to him. 'You know I didn't kill him,' she said, 'you believe that, don't you?'

'Go on,' he said, 'it don't matter a damn what I think, it's what the jury would think that counts.'

She moved away again, and began wandering round the room, fingering the furniture aimlessly as she moved. 'Cattley was a brute. He made me visit him. He gave me the key of his apartment. I had to go to him whenever he called. I knew he had some proof of what I did, so when he was killed, I came down to find it. That's the truth, you do believe that?'

'Sure,' Duffy beamed, 'a hophead would believe it.'

She sat down suddenly in the arm-chair and hid her face in her hands. 'I'm so unhappy,' she said, her voice breaking; 'please be kind to me.'

Duffy came over and sat on the arm of her chair. 'When you went into the Johnny just now,' he said casually, 'you smuggled something in your pants or some place. You can now go right back to the Johnny and dig it out again. Then you can give it to me.'

She took her hands from her face and leant back. Her face was set. 'You've got no right to ask for that,' she said, 'it is nothing to do with you. It is entirely personal.'

Duffy put his arm round the back of the chair and patted her shoulder. 'Go into the Johnny,' he said.

She got out of the chair. Her eyes were very angry. Duffy thought she looked swell. 'I've had enough of this,' she said, speaking very fast; 'I've told you the truth, and I'm not giving you anything. Now, understand that.'

Duffy still sat on the chair-arm. He looked her over slowly, his mouth pursed, and his eyebrows raised. 'You don't seem to understand,' he said; 'I want whatever you found in this joint, and I'm going to have it.'

She started to say something, but he held up his hand. 'Quiet,' he said, 'if you don't like to give it to me, I'll take it, how's that?'

Slowly, she began to back to the door. He could see that she was getting scared. He left his seat quickly as she reached the door, and swung her round. She struck him across his nose with her clenched fist. Duffy was quite hurt. He put his hand to his face, felt his nose gingerly, looked at his fingers to see if his nose was bleeding, then he grinned. 'Well, of course,' he said, 'if that's the way you want it.'

She struck at him again, but he caught her wrist, then she closed with him, a kicking, biting, scratching handful of outraged loveliness. For a moment, Duffy was busy keeping her nails out of his eyes. He smothered her arms with difficulty, turned her. Crossing her arms across her chest, and holding them tightly by the wrists behind her, he ran into the bedroom and slammed her face down on the bed.

'You Redhead,' he said, panting a little with his exertion. 'You going to play ball, or do I have to get rough?'

She said, her voice muffled, 'Oh! How I hate you!'

'Come on.'

She remained silent for a minute, then she said, 'All right, I'll give it to you.'

'That a promise?'

'Yes ... yes, you beast.'

He grunted and released her. She sat up, her face white and drawn. Her eyes were glittering with hate. He was quite startled to see how vicious she could look.

'Get going,' he said, suddenly losing his good temper.

She said, 'Get out of the room. I have to undress.'

He shook his head. 'Be your age,' he said, 'I don't trust you.'

She got off the bed, and stood, her hair ruffled, her green silk dress crumpled, and battle in her eye.

'I'm not getting undressed with a heel like you looking on,' she said.

Duffy went over to the door and turned the key. He took the key out and put it in his pocket.

'You surprise me,' he said, 'fancy you being coy. Sure I'll turn my back, but get going.'

He went and looked out of the window. A very faint sound made him jerk round again. She was almost on top of him. In her hand she was holding an empty carafe by the neck. The look in her eyes made him catch his breath. He slid along the wall away from her fast, as she smashed the carafe at him. The glass exploded all round him. The paper on the wall split, where the carafe had struck, sending a stream of plaster running to the floor.

Her face was contorted with murderous fury. He saw tiny white flecks of foam on her lips. She began to call him filthy names. Hurling them at him, through her twisted mouth.

Duffy thought she must be in a kind of fit. He was so startled that he backed away from her. She advanced slowly towards him, her hands held out in front of her, opening and closing. Every time she closed them, her knuckles stood out white. Then she came at him, like a coiled spring unleashed. Her body struck him with her full weight, and he went back, reeling, off his balance. Her hand shot out and gripped his throat. He could feel the hot burning pain as her long nails dug into his flesh.

Swinging his fist up hard, he hit her on the side of the jaw.

He didn't put any weight behind the blow, but it was a nice smack, all the same. She sagged, fell on her knees, her hands running down his coat front, feebly trying for a grip, then she went forward on her face.

Duffy stepped back and took out his handkerchief. He carefully wiped off his palms, then put the handkerchief back. 'For crying out loud,' he said.

He picked her up and put her carefully on the bed. She lay limp, her eyes closed, breathing hard. He made sure that she was right out, before he began to search her. He didn't like the job, it made him feel like a snake, but he went through with it. Pushed down the top of her girdle, he found what he was looking for. A little red leather note-book. He didn't wait to examine it there and then, he just put it carefully in his inside pocket, rearranged her dress and left her. He let himself out of the apartment, and brought the elevator up from the ground floor. While he waited for it to come up, he kept an ear cocked for any sound from the flat. It was only when he got into the street that he felt at ease. He noticed, across the road, a big Packard was standing. No one was in it. He crossed the road and glanced inside. He recognized the car as the one that had followed him. It belonged to Annabel English.

'Well, well,' he said. This was getting quite beyond him. He walked a little way down the road, then he flagged a cruising taxi. He gave McGuire's address. When the cab jerked off, he settled himself back on the shiny leather, and took out the note-book. It was very neat, each page covered with minute writing. Just names and addresses, and against each name was a number of small denominations. He turned the pages, carefully reading each name, hoping to get some clue. At the fifth page he realized that he was reading down a list of New York's top-liners. He went on. There was no doubt of that. Well-known names began to jump out of the pages. Wives of bankers, stockbrokers, rich playboys, daughters of millionaires, actors and actresses, councillors, a judge here and there, quite a complete list of people in the public eye and who mattered. Duffy looked for Annabel English's name, but he couldn't find it. He held the book in his hand and scratched his head. He thought probably the key lay in the numbers against the names. But it had him beat. He counted the names for something better to do. They totalled just over three hundred. At the end of the book, written faintly in pencil, was a name and address, set apart from the other names. He made it out with difficulty: 'Olga Shann, Plaza Wonderland Club'. He put the note-book in his pocket, and leant back brooding. Perhaps, he thought, he'd get a line from this Olga dame.

The taxi swung to the kerb, and he got out. There was something familiar in the taxi-driver's face. Duffy looked at him hard. The taxi-driver grinned at him.

'You must love that dame,' he observed. 'The last time I brought you to this joint you had to be carried, and now, God love me, she's scratched you to hell again.'

Duffy gave him some money. 'One of these days,' he said evenly, 'someone's going to take a dislike to you.'

The taxi-driver grinned some more. 'I should worry,' he said.

Duffy left him and walked up the steps to the apartment.

CHAPTER SEVEN

When McGuire got in from work, he found Duffy and Alice in the kitchen. Duffy was standing over the stove, a heavy frown on his face, watching a large steak grilling.

McGuire took one look at him and said, 'For God's sake, he's been at it again.'

Alice looked up with a mischievous smile. She was peeling potatoes at the sink. 'He won't say a word.'

Duffy scowled. 'For the love of Mike, pipe down,' he said. 'What if my girl friend did get tough?'

McGuire shook his head sadly. He leant himself up against the wall. 'I never met such a guy,' he said. 'Can't you take care of yourself once in a while?'

Duffy said, 'Know the Plaza Wonderland Club?'

Sam shot a look at Alice. 'I've heard of it.'

Alice said, 'I knew you would. You know all the low clubs.'

Sam protested. 'You got me wrong there,' he said violently; 'I've never been there. I just heard of it from the boys.'

'I know.'

Sam groaned, 'She's always imagining things,' he complained to Duffy. 'As if I'd be seen dead in one of those burgs.'

'You're going to this one tonight,' Duffy said, turning the steak carefully.

Sam cocked his head. 'Is that so?' he said. Again he looked at Alice.

She shrugged. 'I suppose I'll have to say yes,' she said.

Duffy went over and gave her a pat. 'Be nice,' he said. 'This is strictly business. You got to stay home.'

'You men,' she said, but she wasn't mad. Duffy knew she'd take it all right. She was like that. 'Don't get him into trouble,' she said, looking at Sam.

'Me?' Sam laughed. 'I like that. Get him into trouble? It's me that's going to run into that, I bet.'

Duffy shook his head. 'You're just window-dressing,' he said. 'You'll see.'

After the meal, McGuire pushed his chair back and looked inquiringly at Duffy. 'You want to get going?' he said.

Duffy nodded. 'Yeah,' he said. 'Might as well.'

Sam lit a cigarette and went over to get his hat. He slapped it on the back of his head and turned to Alice. 'We ain't going to be late,' he glanced at Duffy, who shook his head. 'Keep the bed warm for me, honey.'

She raised her face to his for a kiss, and Duffy looked on with approval. 'You must've been screwy to marry a tramp like that,' he said to Alice.

Sam grinned. 'There was a shortage of men at the time.'

Alice threatened him with a roll of bread, and he ducked out to get the car.

She said in a small voice, 'You'll be careful?'

Duffy turned his head, and said with elaborate astonishment, 'Why, sure, we're going to have a good time.'

She got up from her chair and walked over to him. 'Save it, Bill. You're poking your nose into this murder business.'

Duffy shrugged. 'This won't amount to much,' he explained.

'I've got a line on Cattley's girl friend. She might turn in some information. This business puzzles me. There is a lot I don't get. Maybe I've been a bit hasty, hiding up that rat. I don't know. This Annabel broad ain't nice. She's dangerous.'

'I wish you hadn't anything to do with it. Sam's worried too.'

Duffy put on his hat. 'I gotta see it through now. Don't you worry about Sam, I won't get him into anything.'

'I'm worrying about you.'

'Forget it,' he pleaded; 'it's going to come out okay.'

She went with him to the door. 'I don't want to be a fuss.'

He patted her shoulder. 'You're swell,' he said. 'It'll be all right.'

He found Sam sitting at the wheel of a small tourer that had seen better days. Duffy climbed in beside him. 'Where's this joint, anyway?' he asked.

Sam let in the clutch with a bang, the car jerked forward, and then stalled. Duffy didn't say anything, he was used to it. Sam pulled the starter, reversed the engine, and let the clutch in again. The car pulled away from the kerb, making a noise like a beehive.

'The Plaza?' Sam said; 'it's near Manhattan Bridge.'

'Know the place?' Duffy asked.

'Sure,' Sam said. 'This is a hot joint. I used to go there a bit in the old days.' Sam always called the time he was single 'the old days'. 'It's tough, and packed with hot pants. You wait.'

Duffy leant back. 'Sounds all right,' he said.

Sam drove two blocks in silence, then he said, 'You telling me the news?'

Duffy gave him a cigarette. 'I looked up Cattley's dump today. Annabel turned up. She was looking for something. She found it, and so did I.' He touched the scratches with his fingers and grinned. 'I bet that honey's as mad as a hornet right now.'

Sam swerved to avoid a big Cadillac, grabbed his handbrake and shouted, 'You street pushover,' to the fat driver.

Duffy took no notice; he had driven with Sam before. 'What did you find?' Sam asked.

'It's a little note-book, full of ritzy names, and it don't mean a thing to me.'

'So?'

'Yeah.' Duffy frowned at his reflection in the driving-screen.
'It's important. I know because I had to get tough with Annabel
to get her to part. That dame scares me. She ain't normal.'

'I thought you liked 'em that way.' Sam looked at him in
surprise.

'Watch the road, dimwit,' Duffy said shortly. 'You ought to
see that dame. When she gets mad, she foams at the
mouth.'

'Yeah?'

'She tried to knock me off,' Duffy said. 'She's screwy. There
can't be any other answer.'

Sam went past the City Hall slowly, then he swung into Park
Row and pushed the pedal down again. 'She needn't be nuts to
want to knock you off,' he said. 'Suppose we stop for a
drink?'

Duffy glanced at the time. It was barely nine o'clock.

'You'll get a drink when we get there,' he said.

The Plaza Wonderland Club was situated on the second
floor, over a hardware store. The entrance was down an alley,
lit with neon lighting. They parked the car and walked up the
alley and went in. At the top of the stairs tickets were being
sold for the taxi-dancers. Duffy bought half a dozen, then they
pushed aside the bead curtains and went into the hall.

There was nothing original about the place. It was dirty and
shabby. The dance floor was small, and you had to step down to
get on to it. Round the floor, tables were crammed together, and
at the far end the girls sat behind a pen. Sam looked across the
room at them and thought they were a pretty swell bunch.

There were very few people at the tables. Just a handful.
They all looked up as Duffy squeezed himself past the tables
and got on to the floor. They watched him cross the floor, with
Sam behind him, and select a table against the wall, opposite
the entrance. He sat down and Sam took the other chair.

The band of three were playing swing music without much
enthusiasm. They plugged away staring with vacant eyes into
space.

'You call this a hot joint?' Duffy said.

'Maybe the depression's hit 'em,' Sam said.

Duffy made frantic signs to a waiter who came over to them with a flat-footed shuffle.

'Let's have a bottle of rum,' Sam said.

'Yeah.' Duffy thought that a good idea. 'Make it a bottle of rum.'

The waiter went off. Duffy said, 'Take a look at this,' he slid the little note-book across the table.

Sam picked it up and studied it carefully. After a little while he handed it back. 'No,' he said, 'that don't mean anything to me. There's plenty of money in that list. I'd say at a guess that little lot's worth a million each. They all belong to the hot set, but that's all I get from it.'

Duffy put the note-book back in his pocket. 'Maybe I'll get a line on it later,' he said.

The waiter brought the rum and set it down on the table with a crisp bang. Sam said, 'This joint's changed.'

The waiter glanced at him. 'Buddy,' he said, 'it's early yet.'

Sam turned to Duffy. 'See?' he said; 'it's early.'

'Okay, it's early. Let's grab a couple of girls, and show them how it's done.'

There was no one dancing on the floor. Sam poured himself out a shot of rum and drank it hurriedly. 'Heck!' he said, 'I believe I'm nervous.'

Duffy looked at him. 'You're kidding yourself, you want to get stewed.'

Sam got up from his chair and wandered across the room to the pen. He stood looking at each girl carefully, until they began to giggle at him. He found a blonde that pleased him and he began to rush her round the empty floor. Duffy picked his girl from where he was sitting, then he went over and dated her up. She was a chestnut red, with a pert little nose and a big, humorous smile. She had a plump, hard little belly that he could feel against his vest. He thought she was cute.

Duffy could dance when he liked, and the rum had made him fairly happy. He swung her round in big smooth circles, and she just seemed to float with him. They didn't say a word through the dance, but when the band cut out, he said, 'You're good.'

She gave him her flashing smile. 'You ain't so bad either.' She got an accent like a heap of tins being tossed downstairs.

He said, 'Come on over and get tight.'

Sam was already there with his blonde. Duffy fancied she smelt, and he sat away from her. Sam liked her a lot. He was showing signs of considerable interest.

Duffy said, 'You girls like rum?'

They both began to protest. They wanted champagne.

Sam shook his head. 'Listen,' he said. 'We're God's gift to womanhood; if rum won't keep you, you can both take a walk.'

Duffy said it was okay with him too.

So they had rum.

The place was crowding up. People kept squeezing between tables. One big chestnut, with large curves, tried to pass Sam, but she couldn't quite make it. Sam looked up, gaped and said, 'Hi, Bill! It's the covered wagon.'

Duffy started to sweat. He guessed Sam was getting drunk.

The chestnut screwed her head round and took a look at Sam, then she laughed. 'You're cute,' she said.

Sam got up and made an elaborate bow. 'Sister,' he said 'you've got it all.'

The chestnut squeezed by, now that Sam stood up. Her escort, a little runt, glared at Sam, who raised two fingers of his right hand.

Duffy said, 'Can't you behave yourself?'

Sam looked grieved. 'She liked it,' he said.

His blonde was looking across the room, tapping her foot. She was annoyed.

Duffy said to the girl with the big mouth, 'Let's dance.'

When they got on the floor he said, 'Olga ain't here to-night?'

She looked up at him, a little frown creasing her brow. 'Olga?' she said.

'Sure, Olga Shann. I'd like to meet her again.'

'She's not here tonight.'

Duffy said, 'Hell, I wanted to talk to that dame.'

They danced in silence for several minutes, then he said, 'Would you like to earn twenty bucks?'

'It's going to cost you a lot more than that.'

Duffy said, 'We're on a different set of rails. I'm offering you twenty bucks for Olga's address.'

She looked disappointed. 'Gee!' she said with a pout, 'I thought we were getting on fine.'

'I'm out on business. I just gotta talk with her.'

She went the length of the room before she said, 'I'll get it for you.'

At the end of the dance she left him. Duffy glanced over at Sam, who was making up to his blonde, so he turned into the toilet. He ran the water and washed his hands. The toilet was empty. It was a small room with cracked tiles half-way up the walls. He dried his hands and dropped the towel into the basket. The door pushed open and a tall man came in. The first thing Duffy noticed about him was his hair. It was jet black, with a broad white streak, running from his forehead to his right ear. It gave his hard face a look of distinction. He wore a close-clipped moustache, and his skin was grey.

Duffy just glanced at him, then made to walk out of the room.

The man said, 'Wait a minute.'

Duffy paused. 'You speaking to me?' he said, surprised.

The man held out his hand. Duffy looked and saw he was holding a .25 automatic.

'You just bought it or something?' Duffy said, suddenly very cautious.

'You got the note-book on you, hand it over.' The man had a curious voice. It was deep-pitched with a little buzz in it.

Duffy said, 'I did have, but it's in the mail now.'

Just then the door opened and Sam came in. The man put his gun away. He didn't seem to hurry, but the gun just disappeared.

Sam said, 'There you are.'

The man looked at Duffy. His pale eyes were very threatening. Then he walked out of the toilet.

Duffy said, 'Who's that guy?'

Sam shrugged. 'Search me,' he said, 'my girl might know.'

Duffy stepped to the door quickly and Sam, a puzzled look

on his face, followed him. 'Did you see that guy come out just now?' Duffy asked the blonde.

She said, 'Sure I did. That's Murray Gleason. Ain't he cute?'

Duffy blotted his face with his handkerchief. 'I couldn't say,' he said, 'we were a bit shy with each other.'

Sam put his arms round the blonde. 'Ain't this a grand place?' he said. He was pretty drunk.

Duffy said, 'I want to get out of here.'

A white-headed little guy came through the hall, heading for the toilet. Sam took the blonde over to him. 'Take care of this baby,' he said. 'Show her round. She's learning in a big way.'

The blonde wrapped the little guy in her arms and began to cry. The rum had her all ends up. Duffy walked out with Sam. The little guy's face was a picture.

Outside, Duffy said, 'You're just hell to go places with.'

Sam waved his hands. 'I guess I'm a little tight,' he said. They walked into the dance-hall again. Sam said suddenly, 'Did that blonde smell a little, or is my nose wrong?'

Duffy said his nose was fine.

The girl with the big mouth was standing by the entrance looking for them. Duffy went over. 'Did you get it?' he asked.

She nodded and gave him a slip of paper, on it was an address. Duffy gave her twenty bucks. She rolled the notes and tucked them in the top of her stocking. Sam leant forward with interest. 'I'm having a swell time,' he said.

Duffy said to the girl, 'I'll be back one of these nights. We'll have a fine time.'

She looked at him wistfully. 'I've heard that before.'

Sam said, 'You're young yet. You'll hear it dozens of times.'

They went downstairs into the street. Duffy stopped at the end of the alley.

'Go home, Sam,' he said. 'Be careful how you drive.'

Sam blinked at him. 'The fun over so soon?' he asked.

Duffy nodded. 'I said you were just window-dressing,' he said briefly. 'I gave you a break. Now go home and look after that wife of yours.'

Sam scratched his head. 'She's probably feeling a little lonesome right now.'

'Get going.'

'Ain't you coming?'

'I'm calling on this Shann broad.'

Sam leered. 'Three being a mob?'

Duffy nodded. 'You got it, soldier,' he said. He watched Sam go over to the parking-place, and then went to the subway on Frankfort Street. Olga Shann had rooms in Brooklyn. He'd never heard of the address, so when he'd got over Brooklyn Bridge he left the subway and flagged a taxi.

He got to the address just after eleven o'clock. He hesitated to ask the taxi to wait. Then making up his mind, he paid him off.

The house was a two-storey villa, with identical models either side, stretching right down the street.

He unlatched the gate and walked up the short gravel path. There was a light showing from one of the second-floor windows. He pressed the buzzer with his thumb, and leant against the wall. He hadn't the vaguest idea what he was going to say.

About three minutes ticked off, then a light sprang up in the hall. He could hear the chain being slipped and then the front door opened. A woman stood there, holding the door only partly open. He couldn't make out her features, she was standing squarely with her back to the light.

'Miss Shann?' he said, taking off his hat.

'Suppose it is,' she said. Her voice had a Garbo tone.

He thought it was a hell of a welcome, but he let it slide. 'It's late for a call,' he said, trying to put his personality across, 'but you'll excuse me, I hope?'

'What is it?'

'I'm Duffy of the *Tribune*,' He took out his Press pass and flashed it, then he put it back again. 'I wanted a word with you about Cattley.'

He saw her stiffen, then she said, 'Let me see that Press card.'

He dug it out again and handed it over. She pushed the door to and examined the card in the light. Then she opened the door wide, and said, 'You'd better come in.'

He followed her into a small sitting-room. It was modern, but the stuff was cheap. He looked at her with interest. The first thing he noticed about her was her eyebrows. They gave her face an expression of permanent surprise. She was lovely in a hard way. Big eyes with long lashes, a scarlet, full mouth; the top lip was almost bee-stung. Her thick chestnut hair was silky and cared for. Duffy liked her quite a lot.

She was wearing a nigger-brown silk dress, tight across her firm breasts and her flat hips.

'Why Cattley?' she said.

He put his hat down on the table. 'This is most unprofessional, but I'm dying for a drink.'

She shook her head. 'Nothing doing.' She was very emphatic. 'Say your piece and get going.'

'My, my,' he said, 'you babes get tougher every day.'

She moved impatiently.

'Okay,' Duffy said hastily. 'I'm looking for Cattley.'

'Why should I know where he is?'

'Why, you're his girl friend, ain't you?'

She shook her head. 'I haven't seen him for months.'

'He thought enough of you to have your name and address in his pocket-book.'

She shrugged. 'Lots of men have girls' names in their pocket-books. It doesn't amount to anything.'

Duffy thought she was quite right. 'Well, well,' he said, 'I guess I've come out of my way.'

She went to the door and opened it. 'I won't keep you,' she said.

Outside, Duffy heard a car drive up. 'You got visitors.'

He saw a startled look come into her eyes, but she said, 'Then you'd better go.'

The buzzer rang loudly. She started a little.

Duffy said, 'Can I go out the back way? I'm feeling I might run into trouble.'

She stood hesitating, then she said, 'Wait here.' Her voice implored him. The buzzer went again, long and insistently.

Duffy said, 'You want me to stay?'

'Yes – I don't know who it is.'

She went out of the room, leaving the door open. Duffy

glanced round, saw another door and went over and opened it. He found himself in a small kitchen. He pushed the door to, and stood looking into the sitting-room, through the small opening.

He heard her at the front door; then he heard her say, 'Why, hello, Max.'

'You alone?' the hoarse voice that spoke made Duffy stiffen. It was familiar. First, he thought it was Joe, but then he knew it wasn't quite like Joe's voice. He'd heard it before.

She said, 'Yes . . . what is it?'

Duffy heard footsteps in the hall and he heard the front door close. 'What do you want?' her voice was nervy and breathless.

A broad-shouldered man, wearing a black slouched hat, walked into the sitting-room. Duffy had him at once. *It was the man who had stolen the camera.*

Duffy clenched his fists. Just the bird he was looking for.

Olga came in and stood by the table. Her face was white and a muscle in her throat fluttered.

'But, Max . . .'

The man glanced round the room suspiciously, then looked at her. His hard eyes raked her from head to foot. 'I ain't seen you for a long time,' he said. 'You're looking swell.' There was no animation in his voice. He sounded as if he were reciting.

She tried to smile, but her lips were frozen. She managed to say, 'That's nice of you.'

He sat himself on the edge of the table and looked at his hands. 'You know Cattley's been knocked off?' he said.

She put her hand to her throat. 'No . . . no, I didn't know that,' she said.

Max raised his head a little and stared at the kitchen door. Duffy stiffened. Then Max said, 'You were sweet on that guy at one time, huh?'

She shook her head. 'He meant nothing to me.'

'So?'

'We went around together, but that's all.'

'You went around together?' He pushed his hat over his eyes. He wouldn't look at her.

'That's right . . . but why . . . why are you asking me?'

'Just curious.' With the flat of his hand he rubbed the short hairs on his nape. 'Did he ever tell you things?'

Duffy could see what a panic she was in. 'He didn't tell me anything . . . he didn't tell me anything . . .'

Max got off the table and went over to the mantelpiece. He examined the photos and fingered the small ivory elephants there. He seemed utterly bored. Then he shrugged. 'I thought maybe he had talked to you,' he said indifferently. He put his hand in the inside of his coat and took out a short silk cord. It was dark red in colour. He dangled it in his fingers.

Olga watched him like a rabbit would watch a snake.

He said, 'This is a pretty thing, ain't it?'

She said, 'What is it?'

'This? Hell, I don't know. I found it.' He continued to swing it in his hand.

She said, 'Did you?'

'I guess I'll scram.' He wandered to the door.

'But . . . but don't you want—?'

'I'll scram,' he said, pausing at the door. 'I thought maybe you'd be interested to hear Cattley's washed up. I see you ain't.'

Her relief was obvious. 'Of course, I'm sorry,' she said, 'but I haven't seen him for so long—'

'That's all right,' he said. 'I liked seeing you.' The flat tone of his voice made the whole thing sound like a badly acted play. He stood on one side at the door and she went ahead to open the front door. When she passed him, he tossed the silk cord over her head with the rapidity of a snake striking, and twisted it round her neck. His knee came up in the small of her back and he threw all his weight on to the cord.

Duffy slipped out of the kitchen like a shadow, and hit Max on his ear with a roundhouse swing. Max, being only on one leg, went over like a felled tree. Olga went on her hands and knees, making a sort of honking sound in her throat.

Max rolled over twice until the wall brought him up, then he dizzily clawed inside his coat for a gun. Duffy whipped up a hall chair and smashed it down on Max. The wall took most of the force, and the back of the chair snapped. Max kicked out at Duffy with a long leg, and his boot caught Duffy on the shin.

Duffy dropped on one knee, his face twisted, and then Max hit him on the side of the head. The blow had no weight behind it, as Max was lying on his shoulder, but it upset Duffy's balance and he went over.

Max again went for his gun and this time he got it out, but Duffy lashed out with his foot and caught Max under the chin. The gun went off with a violent noise. The bullet hit the ceiling, bringing a shower of plaster down on the floor. Max dropped the gun and flopped on his face.

Swearing wildly, Duffy grabbed hold of the gun and scrambled to his feet. He backed away from Max, but the big tough seemed right out. Cautiously, Duffy went over to Olga, who was going blue in the face. He jerked the silk cord loose and helped her to her feet. Her breath still rattled in her throat. He pushed her into the sitting-room.

'Okay, baby,' he said, 'you're all right now.'

He dropped her into an arm-chair. The slamming of the front door brought him out of the sitting-room with an oath. Max had vanished. Outside, he heard a car start up, and by the time he had got to the front door he just caught a glimpse of a tail light vanishing round the bend of the road. He banged the front door to, and went back into the sitting-room. Olga was sitting up feeling her throat. She was crying a little.

'You got any liquor here?' he said.

She pointed to the kitchen. 'It's in the pantry,' she said hoarsely.

Duffy found a big earthenware bottle of apple-jack after a hunt round. He found two glasses and came back into the sitting-room. He filled both glasses and gave her one. 'Put it down,' he said. 'You need it.'

He drained his glass. The apple-jack went down his throat and then when it reached his stomach it exploded. He had to hold on to the table while his head was spinning, and he caught his breath. Just for a moment, he thought he was going to die, then all of a sudden he felt fine.

He looked at the bottle in amazement. 'That's panther's spit okay,' he said.

He filled up his glass again, but this time he was more cautious. He did it in three. He looked at her with a little squint.

'Sister,' he said, 'you're coming home with me. This spot ain't going to be healthy any more.'

The apple-jack was bringing her round. He could see the faint colour coming back to her face. Again she touched her bruised neck. 'I can't do that,' she said.

Duffy went over to her. 'Pack a bag and get going,' he said; 'you gotta make it fast. That bird might come back again.'

Her eyes widened with fear and she got up quickly. He had to help her to the door, her legs were weak. Then, when he saw she could make it, he left her to go upstairs. He went back and gave himself another drink.

By the time she had come down again, he was half cocked. He waved the bottle at her. 'This is the best drop of phlegm-cutter I've run into for some time.'

She stood hesitating on the bottom stair. 'Will you get me a taxi?' she said. 'I'll go to some hotel.'

Duffy went over and took her bag. 'You're coming home with me,' he said. 'For the love of Mike, don't argue.'

He went out in the road and looked up and down, but he couldn't see a taxi. 'We can walk to the end of the road,' he said; 'we'll get a lift there.'

She turned out the lights and slammed the door. They walked down the street together. Duffy felt his feet were pressing into cotton wool. She said nothing until they reached the end of the road, then she said in a small voice, 'Thank you.'

Duffy flagged a cab. He helped her in and gave the driver McGuire's address. Then he got in and sat beside her. He still had the apple-jack in one hand and her suit-case in the other.

'Don't you worry about that, sister. I was so scared I didn't think about you.' He uncorked the bottle, and took another long swig. Then he looked at her suspiciously and said, 'This stuff won't give me Screaming-meemies, will it?'

She turned her face away from him and began to cry.

Duffy fell asleep.

CHAPTER EIGHT

When Sam opened the door and saw them, his eyes popped.

Duffy came into the room, pushing past Sam. Olga hesitated, then followed Duffy. Sam shut the door and stood there scratching his head. He was in green pyjamas and a yellow bathrobe.

Duffy said, 'Don't mind him. He ain't so sissy as he looks.'

Olga gave Sam a scared glance, but said nothing.

Sam said, 'Introduce me, you drunken rat.'

'Miss Shann, this is Sam McGuire.'

She still said nothing.

Alice came out of the bedroom, her dressing-gown wrapped tightly round her. Duffy went over to her. 'This is Olga Shann,' he said. 'She's in a spot of trouble, so I brought her along.'

'Why, of course.' Alice put her hand on Olga's arm. 'Bill can sleep on the couch, you can have his room.'

Olga said, 'But don't you—?'

Duffy put the apple-jack on the table. 'Wait a minute,' he interrupted. 'A nice sleep is what you want, but I've got just a little question to ask you before you go.'

She turned to face him.

'Who was that guy that tried to get tough with you?'

'Max Weidmer. He and Cattley used to work together.'

Duffy nodded. 'Okay; put her to bed, Alice, and be nice to her.'

As Alice led her from the room, Olga said, 'But his face? How did he get so knocked about?'

Sam jerked his head. 'She was talking about you.'

'Know where this Weidmer hangs out?'

Sam frowned. 'Now what?' he asked.

'Come on.' Duffy's face was set.

Sam went to the telephone and spun the dial. While he 'phoned Duffy went into the bathroom and washed his face and hands. Sam came in a moment later. 'He's got a room at the Lexingham Hotel.'

Duffy said, 'Thanks,' then he walked into the sitting-room again.

Sam came in looking lost. 'What's breaking now?'

Duffy said, 'Lend me your rod.'

'Hey! You ain't going to mess around with a heater, for God's sake.'

'Don't talk; I'm getting action. Come on, give me the gun. I want to get going.'

Sam sighed and began taking off his dressing-gown. 'Okay,' he said, 'but I'm coming with you.'

Duffy touched his arm. 'You ain't,' he said. 'Things might happen round this burg. You gotta stay and keep an eye on things.'

Sam screwed up his eyes. 'What *is* this?' he demanded.

'Weidmer tried to twist that dame's neck. He thinks she knows too much. I fancy he might try and get at her here. That's why you stay put.'

Sam's eyes grew big. 'You want to take my gun?' he said 'What about me?'

'Get going,' Duffy said impatiently, 'give me the gun before Alice starts on me. If you drink enough of that panther's breath, you won't need any gun.'

Sam went over to the hall table and came back with a .38 automatic. Duffy took it, looked at the magazine, then stuck it down the waist-band of his trousers. He adjusted the points of his vest to hide the butt.

'I may be late,' he said.

Alice came out just as he stepped into the hall. She just caught a glimpse of him. 'Where's that crazy coon going now?' she asked.

Sam put down the apple-jack hastily. 'He's going to get another dame,' he said wildly. 'He's going to fill the whole goddam house with 'em.'

Alice took his arm. 'You come along,' she said. 'What you need is a good night's sleep.'

She didn't see the worried look in his eyes, as he followed her into the bedroom.

Outside in the street, Duffy flagged a taxi. He gave the driver instructions and then got in the cab. He thought he was spending his life in taxis.

The drive was a long one, and it was just after twelve o'clock when the driver pulled up outside a shabby building.

Duffy paid him off and walked up the steps. The place looked more like a boarding-house than a hotel. He saw a row of letter-boxes and he examined them carefully. Weidmer's name was on the fourth one. Duffy rang the bell at the the top of the row, furthest away from Weidmer's. A moment later he heard the catch being pulled on the front door and he walked in. The hall was lighted by a small gas-burner, and he had just enough light to grope his way upstairs.

On the second floor, he found Weidmer's rooms. He put his hand on the butt of the gun, and then turned the handle. He was surprised to feel the door give. He looked carefully over his shoulder to right and left, then drawing the gun, he stepped quietly into the dark room. He stood in the darkness, listening. There was no sound, except the ticking of a clock somewhere in the room. He just stood, holding his breath, listening. Then, when he was satisfied that the room was empty, he struck a match and lit the gas-burner.

It was a large room, full of shabby furniture. Across the far end stood a bed. Duffy jerked up his gun. There was someone lying face downward across the sheets; it was Weidmer. Duffy moved across the room, his gun steady. But Weidmer was dead. Duffy guessed that before he touched him. He turned him over, and then caught his breath; a big gaping wound showed in Weidmer's throat. Someone had certainly made a job of it, Duffy thought. He released Weidmer, and let him slump back on the bed.

For several minutes, he stood there thinking furiously. Then he began a systematic search of the room. He guessed it would be useless, but he made his search just the same. He couldn't find the camera anywhere. He found one thing that made him blink his eyes. At the bottom of a drawer, he dug out a large glossy photograph. At first glance he thought it was some movie star, then he recognized Annabel English.

'Well, by God,' he said.

Across the photo, scrawled in large sprawling writing, was: 'To dear Max, from Annabel.'

Duffy folded the photo and stuffed it in his pocket. Then he slipped the gun once more down the front of his trousers, and quietly let himself out of the room.

Once more out in the street, he again flagged a taxi and gave Annabel's address. Lying back against the hard seat of the cab, his eyes closed a little wearily, but his mouth was hard and set. He was going to bust the business right on the chin, he told himself.

With the key Morgan had given him, he entered the door leading to the organ loft, and quietly walked up the spiral staircase. When he reached the loft, he found the sitting-room was brightly lit, although no one was visible. He swung his leg over the balcony and lowered himself quietly to the floor.

From across the room he could hear the sound of running water. He thought maybe she was taking a bath. Quietly he began to circulate round the room, opening and shutting drawers. When he came to the wine cupboard he had to kneel down to examine inside. At the back of the cupboard, behind a row of sherry bottles, he found his camera. He took it out and examined it carefully. The first thing he noticed was that the film had been removed. He put the camera in his pocket and shut the cupboard doors carefully.

The bath water had ceased to run, and there was a heavy silence in the apartment. Walking across to the door, he put his hand on the knob and gently turned it, then he walked in.

Annabel was lying in the bath, her eyes closed, smoking a cigarette. Duffy thought she looked swell. He shut the door very gently, and put his back against the panels.

She opened her eyes and looked at him. The only surprise she showed was the way the cigarette slipped out of her mouth. It fell into the water with an angry hiss, then floated down the bath until it rested on her knee. It lay on her knee, looking like some peculiar birthmark. Duffy eyed it with interest.

She shifted one of her feet, causing the water to ripple. 'This calls for a foam bath, don't it?' Duffy said. He went over and sat on the bath stool, that was quite close to the bath. From there he could see the small bruise where he had hit her.

'Get out of here,' she whispered.

He said, 'We're going to have a little talk.' He took from his pocket the camera and showed it to her. Then he produced the photo and showed that to her as well. She lay quite still, her eyes black with hate.

'I know who killed Cattley now,' he said. 'Whoever had the camera rubbed Cattley, I knew that. I had only to find the camera to burst this open. You played your hand very badly, didn't you?'

She said, 'Get out of here, you sonofabitch.'

Duffy's mouth set in a hard grin. 'When I do,' he said, 'the cops are moving in.'

She sat up suddenly in the bath, slopping the water over the edge with her violence. 'You can't pin this on me,' she said; her breathless voice was shrill. 'Find Cattley and see.'

Duffy raised his eyebrows. 'So you shifted him, have you?' he said.

He watched her hand moving slowly over to a transparent bottle, standing on a shelf just above her. He saw it contained ammonia. He took the gun from his waist and showed it to her. 'I'd like to give you another navel,' he said softly. 'Make a move like that and you'll be able to play the penny whistle on yourself.'

Her hand dropped into the water again. He stood up. 'Come out of that,' he said. 'There's lots we got to talk about.'

She climbed out of the bath and grabbed a bath-robe, which she hastily wrapped round herself. Her eyes were like pin-points. Duffy said. 'I'll give you five minutes to fix yourself up, then come out quietly. Don't start anything. I'm leaving the door open.'

He stepped out of the bathroom backwards. A new voice said, 'Drop that gun.'

Duffy stood quite still. The voice said, 'Go on, put the gun on the floor. Don't turn round yet until you've got rid of the gun.'

Duffy put the gun down carefully on the floor at his feet and turned his head. Murray Gleason was standing quite close to him. His hard grey face was cold. He held a Luger in his hand.

Annabel said, 'He knows too much.'

Gleason nodded. 'So it seems,' then he said, 'hurry up and come out. I want you to help me with this bird.'

Duffy stood there, his hands half raised, cursing himself for being so careless. The little note-book burnt in his pocket. It looked as if he were getting into a mighty tight jam.

Gleason said, 'Come away from that gun.'

Duffy turned slowly. 'You don't mind if I sit down?' he said, moving over to an arm-chair. 'Something tells me that I'm going to need a little rest.'

Gleason watched him. 'Don't pull anything,' he said.

Duffy took a cigarette from the box on the table and thumbed the table lighter. He sat down, keeping his hands on the chair arms. He thought Gleason was a trifle jumpy. There was a little twitch going on at the corner of his mouth.

'You've pointed a gun at me before,' he said.

'That was unfortunate. We were interrupted.' Gleason sat on the corner of the table, swinging a long thin foot.

Annabel came out of the bathroom. She stood near Gleason. Her face was very hard, and her eyes were frightened.

Duffy looked at her, then he said, 'What now?'

Gleason said, 'I want that note-book.'

Duffy nodded. 'Sure, I can understand that. I told you before, it's in the mail.'

Annabel said breathlessly, 'He's lying.'

Duffy shrugged. 'You think so? Ask yourself, what would you do? I guessed it was important, so I put it in an envelope and posted it to an address in Canada. When I want it, I just write for it.'

Gleason's eyes narrowed. 'Maybe we could persuade you to write for it.'

Duffy mashed the cigarette into the tray. 'Meaning what?'

'We've got ways . . .'

'Be your age. You can't scare me. Do you think anything you can do to me would pry me loose from something I want? If you want to have that book, talk terms.'

Gleason let the barrel of the Luger fall a shade. It pointed at Duffy's waist coat. 'How much?' he said.

Annabel said, 'You mad?'

Gleason frowned at her. 'Let me handle this.'

Duffy studied his finger-nails. 'What's it worth to you?' he said at last.

Gleason showed his teeth in a little grin. 'I'd pay five hundred dollars for it,' he said casually.

Duffy got to his feet slowly. 'Okay,' he said, 'if that's all you rate it, why bother?'

Gleason jerked up the gun. 'Sit down,' he said, his voice suddenly harsh.

Duffy just looked at him. 'Wake up, louse,' he said evenly. 'You've got nothing on me. That heater don't mean anything now.'

Annabel said with a little hiss, 'Shoot him low down.'

Duffy glanced at her. 'Hell,' he said. 'At one time I got a kick out of looking at you, you murderous little bitch.'

Gleason got to his feet and stood hesitating. His face was almost bewildered. Duffy said to him, 'I'm on my way. When you want that note-book back, give me a ring. I'm in the book.'

Gleason said, 'Wait.'

Duffy shook his head. He wandered to the door. 'You don't get anywhere by letting the gun off. You'll never find the book without me being around.'

Gleason's arm dropped to his side. 'Well, five grand,' he said with an effort.

Duffy shook his head, he opened the door. 'Don't rush it,' he said, 'take your time. Think about it. I'll wait.' He pulled the door behind him and walked to the elevator. He suddenly felt very tired and his brain refused to think. He slid the grille and stepped into the elevator and pressed the ground-floor button.

Outside, he beckoned to a yellow cab, and in a short time he was again climbing the stairs to McGuire's apartment. He opened the door with his key and went in. The clock on the mantelpiece stood at 1.45. He tossed his hat on the sofa and wandered over to the apple-jack, that was still standing on the table. The bottle was light; it was nearly empty. He made a little face. Then he drained the bottle and put it down on the table again. He held his breath for a moment, then gently puffed out his cheeks. The stuff was good.

He stood perfectly still and listened. The apartment was very silent, except for a faint rumbling of Sam's snores. He lit a cigarette and tossed the match into the fireplace, then remembering Alice, he went over and picked it up, putting it carefully in the ash-tray.

With legs that felt rubbery with fatigue, he walked to the spare room and gently opened the door. The room was in darkness. He could hear Olga breathing softly.

He felt his way cautiously to the bed and flipped on the small reading-lamp, then he sat down on the bed gently.

Olga started up, her fists clenched and her lips formed into an 'O'. Duffy put his hand gently on her mouth. 'Okay,' he said softly. 'Take it easy.'

She looked at him and then lay back. 'You scared me silly,' she said.

'Quiet,' he said, 'I don't want the others to wake.'

She looked from him to the clock and then back at him again. 'It's so late . . . what is it?'

'Things are happening,' he said. 'I gotta talk to you. You know the spot you're in, don't you? Max has been knocked off. Someone paid him a visit and slit his throat for him.'

The pupils of her eyes became very big. 'You mean—?'

'I'm going to start from the beginning. Then you gotta fill in the gaps.' He lay back a little, resting on his elbow. His battered face was drawn with fatigue. She suddenly felt a little pang of compassion for him.

'Take off your shoes and lie here beside me.'

He shook his head. 'I'd go to sleep,' he said. 'Now listen. There's a redhead called Annabel English, she's the daughter of Edwin English, the politician. She's wild and bad. One of her boy friends is this guy Weidmar. She has dealings with Cattley. This punk called on her and she tossed him down the elevator shaft. Right, before we go any further, you gotta tell me all you know about Cattley.'

She said in a low voice, 'Cattley was mixed up in a big dope traffic. He started off in a small way, peddling the stuff and taking a rake-off. That was when I knew him. Then he got big and began to make money. Weidmer was his boss. Gleason was the big shot. Cattley got tired of taking orders and he stole the list of customers—'

'Stop!' Duffy's voice sounded like the snap of a steel trap. He took the little note-book from his pocket and put it on the coverlet before her. 'Is this the list?'

Her startled face told him. 'So that's it,' he said. He thumbed the book through. 'Why, these guys can't operate without this list . . . the dope buyers must be hopping mad.' He shut his eyes and tried to think.

'How . . . how did you get that?' she asked.

He opened his eyes. 'I got it from Cattley's joint. Annabel came down to look for it, and I took it off her. This makes things pretty clear. Hell! They certainly operated in a big way. Look at those names, for God's sake.'

She put her hand on his arm. 'They'll get it away from you,' she said, fear coming into her eyes. 'It means millions to them.'

Duffy turned on his elbow and looked at her. His tired eyes searched her face. 'You know,' he said, speaking slowly, 'years ago, I used to think of being in a spot like this. To have the chance of grabbing a million dollars from a bunch of toughs. Well, I've got my chance. I'm going to play the ends against the middle.'

'What do you mean?'

'If they find you've squawked, you're going to be washed up. I like you, honey. Will you come in on this with me?'

Her eyes became shrewd again. 'How?'

'This guy Morgan,' Duffy said, 'you ain't heard about him. I can't quite see how he fits, except he's looking for easy dough.'

She looked blank. 'Morgan?'

Quickly and with economy, he told her about Morgan and the three toughs. 'They thought they'd blackmail Annabel. It'd be good enough to publish a photo of Cattley and Annabel to upset old man English. I thought it was deeper than that. Gee! I gave her the benefit and thought they killed Cattley to pin it on her. All the time she had killed Cattley herself, and I was sucker enough to help her shift the body. Anyway, that's her funeral now. I'm selling the book to the highest bidder.'

Olga said, 'Why should Morgan want to buy it?'

Duffy grinned. 'Use your head,' he said. 'This crowd here,' he tapped the note-book, 'is lousy with dough. They'd pay any-thing to hush up scandal. How'd it look if it got round that they traded in dope?'

She leant back in the bed and brooded. Then she said, 'I believe you've got something.'

Duffy put the note-book away. 'You bet I've got something,' he said. 'Why not? Why the hell shouldn't I make a little dough out of these punks? Why shouldn't you?'

'How much will it be?' she asked.

'Fifty grand, hundred grand, anything.'

She lay back flat, and ran her fingers through her thick hair. Duffy thought she was a very nice broad indeed. 'We could do a lot with that money, couldn't we?' she said, her voice thrill-ing.

Duffy patted her hand. 'Yeah,' he said, 'we could do a lot.' He glanced at the clock and got stiffly to his feet. 'I'm going to have a little sleep. There's action coming.'

She put her hand on his arm. 'You look so tired,' she said.

He dug up a grin. 'You're dead right, sister.'

She lay there, her eyes very bright, and he could see the sudden rising and falling of her breasts under the sheet. She said, looking into his eyes, 'I could make you better. Won't you come?'

He sat down on the bed again. 'You're swell,' he said. 'Not tonight. Tomorrow we'll get out of here.' He paused, then he nodded his head to the next room. 'They're nice people. It wouldn't be fair on them. Tomorrow.'

He put his hand against her face. 'Didn't you think Alice was swell?' He stepped away from the bed. 'They mustn't know about this. This is between you and me.'

She watched him go from the room, then turned out the light. She lay in the dark a long time, before she fell asleep.

Part Two

IT FINISHES

CHAPTER NINE

Duffy stepped into Ross's garage and looked round the dim shed. Ross came out of the little office at the far end of the shed. He was big and fat, with a glistening rubbery face. He plodded over the oily concrete, waving a short thick arm.

'Don't tell me,' he wheezed when he saw Duffy. 'Let me guess.'

Duffy drew his lips off his teeth in a mirthless grin. 'Ain't seen you for years,' he said.

'I bet you're in a jam.'

Duffy shook his head. 'You're wrong,' he said. 'It ain't anything like that. I want to spend some dough with you.'

Ross put his broad hand on Duffy's arm. 'Well, well,' he began, leading Duffy to the office. 'I've got a bottle in there that'll suit you.'

Duffy sat down in a basket chair and looked round the small box-like room. Ross nearly filled it.

'Gettin' mighty hot, ain't it?' Ross said, bringing out a black bottle from his desk cupboard. He wiped the mouth of the bottle on his shirt-sleeve and pushed it over to Duffy. 'You be careful of that liquor,' he went on, 'that's Tiger's sweat okay.'

Duffy took a swig, rolling the liquor round his mouth before swallowing. Then he grunted a little. 'Yeah,' he said, 'it's fierce.'

Ross took the bottle from him and raised it to his lips. Duffy watched his Adam's apple jump in his fat throat. Ross put the bottle on the table, wiped his wet mouth on the back of his hand, and hitched his chair forward a little. 'Now, what's the business?'

Duffy lit a cigarette and rolled another across the table to Ross. 'You still got that old Buick around?' he asked.

Ross's little eyes opened a trifle. 'You mean the armoured one?'

'That's it.'

Ross nodded. 'Sure I've got it.'

'Does she run?'

Ross grinned. 'Does she run? Listen, all my cans run. That bus's as good as new.'

Duffy said, 'I want to rent her for a bit.'

Ross shrugged. 'That's okay,' he said simply. 'Why not have my Packard? Now that's a swell job.'

Duffy shook his head. He got to his feet. 'I want the Buick,' he said. 'I might need a little protection from now on, and I'd feel a lot safer in the Buick.'

Ross said, 'I knew it, you're in a jam.'

'Show me the wagon.'

Ross led him out into the shed again. 'That's her.'

The Buick was just an ordinary-looking car, slightly shabby in the body, although she had been freshly washed down. Duffy looked her over thoughtfully. 'Sell her to me,' he said at last.

Ross took a quick look over his shoulder, then plodded over. 'She looks the berries, don't she?' he said. He opened the door. 'You try that.'

Duffy had to make a strong effort to get the door to shut. 'That's steel,' Ross said. 'Good thick stuff, see?' He opened the door again and climbed inside. Duffy leant against the door and put his head forward.

'The guy that threw this bus together knew all about it,' Ross said, settling his hindquarters firmly on the padded seat. 'The roof is armour plate. Take a look at the windows.' He rolled one down. 'Looks all right from the outside, but see how thick they are.'

The glass was at least three-quarters of an inch in thickness.

'That'll bounce a .45 slug back at the guy who sent it,' Ross said. He touched a spring in the dashboard and a small panel slid back. He put his hand inside and took out two Colt automatics. You won't need these,' he said. 'I'll clear them out for you.'

'Let 'em stay, they can go with the bus,' Duffy said quietly.

Ross looked at him, pursed his fat mouth, then shrugged. He put the guns back. 'Under the seat there's four hundred rounds.'

Duffy said, 'For the love of Mike.'

Ross grinned. 'I ain't had time to shift the stuff. It's been in there some time.'

'It's a fine job. Anything else?'

Ross climbed out of the car again. 'The radiator grill is bullet-proof. The engine is protected with plate. The rear window rises from the bottom, so you can operate a gun if you wanted to. And the tyres are filled with puncture-healing liquid which fills any holes immediately if a slug finds its way there. That cab is certainly a swell job for trouble.'

Duffy pushed his hat to the back of his head. 'Yeah, I guess it's right up my street. What you want for her, Ross?'

Ross scratched his bald head. 'What you got, buddy?' he asked. 'You done things for me in the past . . .'

Duffy said, 'I'll give you thirty bucks a week for her.'

Ross shook his head. 'Too much,' said. 'I'll take twenty.'

Duffy took forty dollars from his pocket-book and handed them over. 'I'll take her for a couple of weeks,' he said. 'Fill her up, will you?'

Ross pushed the money into his trouser pocket. 'She's ready to go.'

Duffy opened the door and got in. 'I'll be seeing you, pal,' he said.

Ross put his fat face through the window frame. 'Take it easy with the cannons,' he said anxiously. 'They ain't registered, but take it easy all the same.'

Duffy nodded at him and engaged the clutch. The Buick rolled out into the street. Duffy drove to his bank, cashed a cheque for a thousand dollars, checked his deposit and went back to the car again. With the thousand on him, and three thousand in the bank, he could last a little while, he thought.

Olga was waiting for him at 'Stud's Parlour', a quiet little bar just off East 164th Street. When he drove up, she ran out and he pushed open the off door for her. She got in, and he had to lean over her to slam the door shut. 'That's stiff,' she said.

'It's steel,' he grinned, pulling away from the kerb. 'This tub's from Chi. They know how to build 'em there.'

She was silent for a half a block, then she said, 'You expecting trouble?'

'Trouble'll blow up sooner or later in a racket like this. I like to be prepared for it.' He pushed the Buick past a big truck, then he said, 'You ain't going to get scared?'

She shook her head. 'I don't scare easily.' She put her neat gloved hand to her throat. She was wearing a high-necked blouse. 'Your friends were swell,' she said as an afterthought.

Duffy nodded. 'I'm a heel all right,' he said. 'I told Alice I was seeing you on the train for your home.'

Olga said, 'You couldn't let them in on this?'

Duffy shook his head. 'They've got each other. They don't give a damn for money; why should they? It's punks like you and me that ain't got anchors that think money's the tops.'

She shot a quick glance at him. 'You're not feeling sore?' she ventured.

Duffy shook his head again. 'No, not sore. I've started this, so I'm finishing it. If I don't get away with it, it don't matter. If I do, well, I'll spend what I get, and think I'm having a swell time.'

She said in a low voice, 'And me?'

Duffy put his hand on her knee. 'You're okay, baby, you'll get what you want.'

He pulled up outside his apartment. 'Come on in and see how you like your new home.'

They went upstairs, and she stood waiting for him to open the door. Inside the small apartment they stood and looked at each other, then she turned her head quickly and walked over to the window. 'I like this,' she said. 'It's nice, isn't it?'

Duffy threw his hat on the chair and brought out a bottle of rum. 'You like Bacardi?' he said.

'Yes, but it's early yet, isn't it?'

Duffy took two glasses and poured out the rum. He went over to her and put the glass in her hand. 'To you and to me and to dough,' he said.

The Bacardi went down smooth, leaving a hot ball of fire burning inside them.

'Take your hat off, honey,' he said, 'this is your home now.'

She said, 'Is that the bedroom over there?'

'That's it. Go ahead and have a look.' He was surprised to find his hands were trembling. He watched her walk slowly across the room and into the bedroom. Her long legs and flat hips had a lazy movement, but there was an electric tension that radiated from her.

He followed her and stood just behind her, looking at her in the mirror. She raised her eyes, studied his face, then she turned quickly.

He put his hands on her hips and drew her to him. 'You're swell,' he said. 'I've known you twenty-four hours, but it seems a lifetime. I bet you're bad. I bet you've loved, but I don't care.'

She said, 'I've been all that and more.' She took his hands in hers, held them for a moment, then pushed them away from her. She went over to the bed and sat down.

Duffy shifted away from the mirror and leant over the back of the bed. 'We've got to get together,' he said. 'Tell me about yourself.'

She turned her head and looked at him. 'Isn't it unwise?' she said.

Duffy shook his head. 'I want to know,' he said.

'I was born in a small Montana town.' Her voice was flat and expressionless. 'Living there was like living in a morgue. Nothing ever happened. The sun shone, the dust collected on the dry roads, carts came and went, nothing ever happened. I used to get fan magazines and read about Hollywood. Millions of other girls have done the same. I thought if I got to Hollywood, I'd get a break. I dreamed Hollywood, lived Hollywood, and I guess I even slept Hollywood. Well, one day I took my chance. I waited until my Pa had gone into the fields, then I took all his money – it wasn't much – and I blew. I never got to

Hollywood. My dough gave out when I hit Oakland. I got a job as a hostess in a dance hall there.'

Duffy came round and sat on the bed close beside her.

'I had to be nice to the men at the bar. Talk to them, kid them along, and get them to buy drinks. They paid me commission on the drinks. It didn't last long. The boss called on me one night, and then I hadn't anything to take care of after he had been over me. Well, you know how it is, once on the slide, you can't stop.'

Duffy said, 'How long ago was this?'

'About eight years. I was seventeen then. I ran into a guy named Vernor. How that guy kidded me! He certainly could paint a picture. He showed me how I could make money so fast that I'd get dizzy. Pretty clothes, motor-cars, jewellery, and all the rest of it. Just by selling myself three or four times a night. I fell for it. What did it matter, so long as I could get enough dough to get out of the game in a year or so?

'He got me into a house in Watsonville, one of the northern Californian towns, and once I was there I knew what a sucker I'd been. I just couldn't get away. They never gave me any money. They kept my clothes from me. They threatened me with the police; in fact, they had me.'

Duffy grunted, 'A sweet life you've had.'

She was silent for a moment, then she went on. 'I didn't see a white man for three years. Filipinos, Hindus and Chinks, yes, but no white man.'

Duffy moved restlessly. He didn't like this.

'Just when I was giving up, along came Cattley. Can you imagine that? Cattley came into my room, and I was expecting another of those fierce little brown men. Cattley fell for me, and I gave him everything I had. He thought I could be useful to him, so he got me out of the place and set me up in that little house.'

Duffy said, 'How could you be useful to a guy like Cattley?'

Her face hardened a little. 'I'm telling you everything, aren't I?' she said.

Duffy leant back on his elbows. 'Sure, and it don't sound so good.'

She lifted her shoulders wearily. 'It isn't good. In Cattley's business he had to have a woman around. He got me to play hostess to his suckers. I got him introductions to the upper set. It was through me that he made so much money. Cattley was on the level with me. He gave me plenty.' She sighed, twisting her hands. 'Now the poor mug's dead.'

In the other room the telephone began to ring. Duffy made no move to answer it.

Olga said, 'What's the matter? Don't you want to answer it?'

'Let it ring,' he said, 'looking at her.

The telephone stopped ringing.

She stood facing him, then she said, 'Yes . . . yes . . . yes.'

He reached out and pulled her roughly to him. 'I'm crazy about you,' he said, his lips hard against her throat.

The telephone began to ring again. It rang for a long time, then it stopped. A fly buzzed busily from room to room, hitting the window with distinct little plops.

On the bed, Duffy lay, his eyes half shut, feeling the muscles of his body running into liquid. Olga went to sleep. Duffy watched her. Time meant nothing to him. He was quite content to look at her. Her body was strong and white. Her flesh was firm. He thought she looked good.

He put out his hand gently and touched her hair. She stirred and opened her eyes. She smiled at him.

Duffy said, 'You've got me. You've got me hard.'

'I want to go away with you,' she said, putting her hand on his arm. 'I want to get away from all this. You won't let me down, now?' She said 'now' very urgently.

Duffy shook his head. 'It'll be all right, you see.'

The telephone began to ring insistently.

Olga sat up. A little shiver ran through her. She said, 'No, don't go. Leave it.'

Duffy hesitated, then got off the bed. He looked at her for a moment, smiled, then went into the other room. He took the receiver off the prong.

'What is it?' he said sharply.

'Gleason talking,' came the harsh purring voice.

Duffy pulled a chair up and sat down. His eyes and mouth

were suddenly hard. 'Okay,' he said, 'I didn't expect you so soon.'

'I've been ringing for some time.' There was just a hint of nerves in Gleason's voice.

'Well, you got me now.'

'I'll buy that thing from you for fifteen grand,' Gleason said with a rush.

Duffy grinned into the 'phone. 'I must be getting deaf,' he said. 'It sounded like you said fifteen grand.'

Gleason was silent for a minute, then he said, 'I can't go higher than that. Fifteen grand.'

'What the hell kind of a cheap punk are you? Ain't you aching to get that list back? The list is worth that much as State evidence.'

'Now listen,' Duffy could almost see Gleason squeezing the telephone with excitement, 'I can't lay my hands on any more dough. I'll make you a fair offer. Fifteen grand and five per cent cut on the business.'

'Aw, use your head,' Duffy shifted forward in his chair a little. 'I ain't so dumb. What's five per cent cut to a corpse? I wouldn't trust you, Gleason, for a second. Once you had that list, you'd bust your guts to iron me out. No, it's cash or nothing.'

Gleason said, 'You goddam sonofabitch.'

'Skip it. You don't know what you're up against. I've got another buyer in the market. You're going to pay plenty for that list, or the other guy gets it.'

There was a heavy silence at the other end, and Duffy reached over for a cigarette. He had nothing to do, and plenty of time to do it in.

Then Gleason said, 'That's the way you're going to play it, huh?'

'You got it. Ends against the middle. I ain't in a hurry, but you'd better start revising your ideas.'

'You're going to find yourself in a heap of trouble,' Gleason said. His voice was suddenly steady. He seemed no longer excited. 'I'd play ball on the level, Duffy, or . . .'

'Listen, you yellow punk, you can't throw a scare into me. I know just where I've got you. Start the bidding at fifteen grand if you like, but the price is going to the roof.' He dropped the receiver back on the prong and sat back.

Olga came out of the bedroom. She was still nude. 'Are you handling this right?' she asked.

Duffy went over to her and put his hands round her back. 'This is the way it's going to go,' he said. 'It'll take a little time, but it'll yield the most dough.'

She looked up into his face. 'Can't you trust him?'

Duffy shook his head. 'It's going to be tricky getting away with the dough,' he said, 'but you watch me, we'll beat 'em.'

She leant against him. 'I didn't care what happened, but I do now. I don't want you to get into a jam after this.'

He led her back into the bedroom. 'Put on a wrap,' he said. 'I can't think with you like that.'

He watched her undo the small case she had brought with her, and find a wrap, then he helped her put it on.

They went back into the sitting-room again. Olga lit a cigarette, drawing down the smoke and holding it. She said, 'You're hatching something, what is it?'

Duffy took from his inside pocket a little note-book and put it on the table. Then he brought out another book, identical with the first. He laid it beside the other.

Olga looked at them closely, then released a cloud of smoke down her nostrils. 'A double-cross,' she said.

'You've got it.' Duffy drew up a chair and sat down. I'm showing you how dough's made.' He took out a fountain-pen and began to copy the list of names from the first book into the second.

She sat on the edge of the table and watched him.

'Someone's going to get mighty sore about this,' she said at last.

Duffy didn't look up. He went on writing, but he said, 'We won't be there to see 'em.'

When he had finished the list, he went back again to the beginning and studied the pages. 'You know what these numbers stand for? Look, Max Hughson 5. Johnny Alvis 7. Trudie Irvine 4.'

She leant over his shoulder. 'Payments,' she told him.

'Hughson used to pay five thousand dollars a month for his dope and protection.'

'That's plenty. Why protection?'

Olga swung her long legs. 'That was Gleason's way. These birds aren't real hopheads. They just play at it. Gleason sold them the dope, then warned them that someone was on to them, and it would cost them so much to hush it up. He only had to put the screw on a little, scare them to hell, and show them that he could warn off all comers, to get himself put on their pension list.'

Duffy did sums, then he looked up. 'This little book is worth five hundred grand to a cool million, if they all pay.'

Olga nodded. 'When I was with Cattley and he was working it, they mostly did pay,' she said.

Duffy grinned. 'It's easy to make money, if you know how,' he said, getting to his feet. 'Well, we'll see what Morgan's got to say.'

She slid off the table. 'What are you doing with the books?' she asked.

'You shall have one and I'll have the other.' He gave her the copy. 'Be careful with that.'

She held the book in her hand for a moment, looking at him very hard, then she smiled and put the book in his hand.

'What's this?'

She said, 'I hoped you would do that. I just wanted to see if you trusted me. It's screwy to keep this where it could be lifted. Keep it.'

He said, 'Well, I'll be goddamned.' But she looked so pleased that he took the book and put it with the other in his inside pocket.

She said, 'You're not going to Morgan alone. I'm coming with you.'

He thought for a moment, then he nodded. 'Oke, but you stay outside in the bus. We'll plant the lists at my bank on the way down.'

She ran into the bedroom to change. Duffy called to her. 'I'll get Morgan's address from the *Tribune*. They'll be bound to know it.'

While he 'phoned, he vaguely heard her in the bathroom, and

when he had got the address from the reporters' room, he wandered in. She was standing under the cold shower, holding her face up to the tingling pin-points of water. Her eyes were closed, and she held her breasts cupped in her hands.

Duffy leant forward and turned the wheel on hard. The cold water struck her fiercely, and she ducked away, gasping. Duffy grabbed a towel and wrapped her in it.

'Get busy,' he said, 'we ain't got all day.'

She mopped her face, then stepped out of the bath. 'Try it,' she said, 'it's nice.'

Duffy shook his head. 'Later,' he said. 'I've got the money itch.'

She took off the rubber cap that protected her hair and threw it at him. The drops of water splashed his face. Duffy aimed a smack at her, then he jerked her to him and kissed her.

He thought, 'We're behaving like a couple of kids.'

She said, looking up at him, 'Will you always be kind to me?'

He gripped her arms suddenly, hurting her. 'Let's go,' he said, 'there's work to be done.' And he left her, standing quite still, holding the towel round her, with a little bewildered look in her eyes.

CHAPTER TEN

Duffy left the Buick at the kerb and climbed the five flat steps to the front door. Morgan's house was in a big way. Duffy was quite surprised. He expected something good, but this was a lot better than good.

The front door was a plate-glass affair, plastered with wrought iron. The bell had to be reached for and pulled down, like the plumbing in an old-fashioned toilet.

Duffy called back to Olga, who was sitting in the car, 'Some joint'. He selfconsciously jerked the bell-pull hard.

Clive opened the door.

Duffy said, 'Tell your Queen I want to see him.'

Clive threw up his hands and backed away from the door. He said in a shrill voice, 'You get out . . .' Duffy pushed the door wide open, but he stayed where he was. He said in a level voice, 'Get going or I'll start on you.'

Clive slid his hand inside his coat, and Duffy took a quick step forward and smacked Clive across the face.

The little guy said from the head of the stairs, 'Don't hit him again. He'll be all right.'

Clive took his hand away from his coat and backed farther away. A high whinnying sound was coming from his mouth. Duffy said, 'Why don't you take this bum away?'

The little guy came down the stairs. He wore his hat pulled down. Duffy couldn't imagine him without that hat.

Duffy said, 'Where's Morgan?'

The little guy was very cautious, he did not get too close to Duffy. He said with a thin smile, 'You surprised him.'

Duffy said, 'I don't care about that. I came to see Morgan.'

The little guy turned his head to speak to Clive. 'You heard him?' he said. 'He came to see Morgan.'

Duffy reached forward and grabbed the little guy by the coat-front. His eyes were like granite. 'Cut this circus stuff of yours out.'

The little guy pushed an automatic hard into Duffy's vest. 'Don't get tough, Mister,' he said.

Duffy took his hand away, and stepped back a little. He said, 'Put that rod up and use your head.'

The little guy said to Clive, 'Tell Morgan.'

Duffy stood there watching the little guy thoughtfully.

The little guy said hopefully, 'You ain't going to start trouble, are you?'

Duffy shook his head. 'Your daffodil went for her gun,' he said. 'I wouldn't stand for a thing like that.'

The little guy giggled. 'You'd like Clive once you got to know him,' he said.

Duffy still stood motionless. 'Suppose you put that heater away,' he said evenly. 'This ain't the time for pop-guns.'

The little guy shoved the gun into his shoulder-holster. 'I get nervous sometimes,' he said, waving his hands apologetically.

A door at the end of the hall opened and Morgan came out. He called, 'Come in here.'

Duffy walked the length of the hall slowly. Then he entered the room. Morgan was standing just inside. Across the room, Joe leant against the wall, chasing holes in his teeth with a wooden pick.

Duffy nodded at Morgan.

Joe said, 'Why, for the love of Mike, here's the pip back again.'

Morgan half raised his hand, stopping Joe. He said, 'Have you brought the photos after all, Mr. Duffy?'

Duffy said, 'Clear your thugs out, I want to talk to you.'

'Shall I pat him around?' Joe asked. 'He likes it, and can he take it?'

Morgan said, 'Wait outside.'

Joe shrugged, but he went out, passing close to Duffy. As he passed, he pushed his flat face into Duffy's and grinned. 'Nice boy, ain't you?' he said.

Duffy didn't move. 'Your breath's bad,' was all he said.

Joe shut the door behind him, then Duffy walked over to a big arm-chair and sat down. He didn't remove his hat. Morgan leant against the overmantel and waited.

'We're due for a talk, ain't we?' Duffy said.

Morgan took out a cigar case, selected a long thin Havana, put it between his small teeth, bit off the end neatly and spat the end into the empty grate. He put the cigar case back in his pocket.

Duffy said, 'I'll smoke too.'

Morgan looked at him. His hooded eyes were very hostile. 'Not mine, you won't. You talk.'

Duffy shrugged and took a cigarette from his case. 'If that's how you feel . . .'

Morgan hid his face behind thick smoke as he lit the cigar. 'You've still got five hundred bucks of mine,' he said.

Duffy nodded. 'Sure,' he took his wallet out and counted out five one-hundred bills, then tossed them on the table. 'I've been keeping them for you.'

Morgan's face was quite blank. He looked hard at the five bills, then he put his hands behind him, and raised himself slightly on his toes. 'That came as a surprise,' he said, 'I thought you were taking me for a ride.'

Duffy said, 'That's scent money; buy your nance a present.'

Morgan stiffened. 'You watch your mouth,' he said in a thick voice.

'Let's skip this, and get down to things. I've been wanting a talk with you for some time. When you sent me out on that phoney photo stunt of yours, I fell right into trouble, and I've been that way ever since. I'm getting to like it, and I'm seeing quite a bit of dough hanging to it. You play ball with me now, and you're going to get into something that's going to make your ears flap. Let's get this straight. You wanted to put the screws on Edwin English, through his daughter, ain't that the way it goes?'

Morgan stared at him for several minutes, his eyes expressionless, then he said, 'Suppose it was?'

'If I'd turned in those photos of Cattley and the girl together, you could have cracked down on English. You could have warned him off your rackets, and he would have had to like it.'

Morgan wandered over to a chair and sat down, but he didn't say anything.

'You know Murray Gleason?'

A flicker of surprise went over Morgan's face. 'Yeah, I know him.'

'What do you know about him?'

'Where's this leading?' Morgan was suddenly impatient.

'I'll tell you. Gleason is running a big dope racket amongst some of the real big shots in the upper circle. He's got them so short that they're screaming murder. That guy has a pension from them of nearly a million bucks. Did you know that?'

Morgan shook his head. His thick lips curled a little. 'That ain't true,' he said. 'Gleason is only a cheap peddler – was when last I knew him.'

Duffy laughed. 'You're out of date,' he said. 'Gleason's moved into the big-shot class, but he's smart enough to keep it to himself. He stands no chance of having any political boss smacking his ears down for him.'

Morgan said at last, 'I ain't interested in Gleason.'

Duffy nodded. 'Sure you ain't,' he agreed, 'but you'd like his racket, wouldn't you?'

'When I want his racket I'll take it,' Morgan said, tapping the long ash into the tray.

Duffy leant back and studied the ceiling. 'Gleason's had a list of all his customers and the amounts they pay for protection,' he said.

Morgan looked up sharply. 'You said "had"?'

Duffy still didn't take his eyes from the ceiling. 'Sure, that's right. I've got it now.'

Morgan sat silent, then he said, 'I see.'

Duffy said, 'It's in the market right now.'

Morgan became elaborately casual. Duffy nearly laughed at him. 'It might be useful,' he said.

Duffy said, 'You ain't got the idea quite.' He spoke carefully, as if to a child. 'This English girl is tied up with Gleason. She's as wild and crazy as a loon. These two are working this racket between them. And they're making plenty out of it. With the list, you can smash their little game, put English on the spot, and have three hundred big shots pouring their dough into your lap, just to keep out of it.'

Morgan chewed on his cigar. 'The way you're putting it, it sounds good,' he said.

'It is good. That's why I'm offering it to you.'

'What have I done?'

'You got the dough.'

'How much?'

'Fifty grand,' Duffy said. 'I don't mean thirty, or forty. It's worth fifty, and it's fifty I want.'

Morgan shrugged his shoulders slightly. 'I guess you'd never peddle that for that amount of dough,' he said.

Duffy stood up. 'Okay,' he said, 'I'll get the money from the other side. Why should I worry?'

'Wait. You've overlooked something.' Morgan looked foxy. 'You've given me some nice information. I don't doubt that. Think, would you pay that much money? You forget, I've got three guys who're eating their heads off for a job. I ain't paying fancy prices for a thing like that. Do you know what I'd do if I had a list like that?'

Duffy said, 'What would you do?'

Morgan grinned. He looked like a wolf. 'What you've done. Make a duplicate and sell it to both sides.'

Duffy's face was quite blank. 'It's an idea,' he said, considering it.

Morgan shook his head. 'It was a pip of an idea, but not now When you've sold that list to Gleason, I'll call on him and take it away from him.'

Duffy said, with a hard smile, 'You're pretty sure of yourself, ain't you?'

Morgan raised his fat shoulders again. 'And I'll tell you something else,' he went on, flicking his ash into the tray, 'I'll send Joe to collect that fifty grand off you, when Gleason has paid it. That ought to show you.'

Duffy moved to the door. 'I guess you and I won't get on so well in the future,' he said sadly. 'I'm sorry about that.'

'You will be,' Morgan said very gently.

Duffy opened the door. Joe was standing just outside. Duffy looked over his shoulder at Morgan. 'There ain't anything more now, is there?'

Morgan shook his head. Then a thought crossed his mind and he said, 'Wait.'

Duffy stood still. He didn't turn his back to Joe, but stood three-quarters, so that he could watch Joe from the corner of his eye. 'Yeah?' he said.

Morgan picked up the five bills from the table. 'Suppose you take these and give me the list?'

'What for?' Duffy was quite startled.

'You can't break into the game,' Morgan said. 'You're soft. What've you got that'll stand up against an outfit like mine? Get wise to yourself, you little heel. Where's the dough coming for your protection? Who's going to work for an out-of-work button-pusher? You must be nuts to come to me with a proposition like that. Here, give me the list and take the five hundred bucks. That's what you're worth, and save yourself a lot of grief.'

Duffy's expression didn't change, but his eyes went suddenly frosty. 'Soft? Was that it?' he said.

Morgan shrugged. 'I've wasted enough time with you. Scram, I'll do the job myself.' He put the five bills into his pocket. Then he looked up quickly. 'I want that list tonight,' he said evenly. 'You can't buck the rap. The list tonight, or I'll turn Joe loose on you.'

Duffy nodded; he stepped past Joe carefully, who grinned at him, then he walked to the front door and down the steps.

Olga looked at him and said, 'So it didn't work.'

Duffy engaged the gear and drove the Buick down the block. He began to swear softly under his breath, without moving his lips. Olga laced her fingers round her knees and stared ahead.

Duffy swung the Buick into Seventh Avenue and went with the traffic. He cut right at Longacre Square and drove into Central Park. When he reached the lake, he stalled the engine and stopped.

Olga said, 'Don't get mad.'

For a moment he said nothing, then he took off his hat and tossed it at the back of the car. 'Those birds certainly got me going,' he said. A grim little smile came to his mouth, and she liked him a lot better.

'Tell me,' she said.

He screwed round in his seat, so that he was facing her, and took her gloved hands in his. 'This is going to get tough,' he said. 'You'd better skip before the war starts.'

Her eyes narrowed slightly. 'Suppose you cut out the hysterics and tell me.'

Duffy said, 'Morgan wants the list. I'm to hand it over tonight or else . . .'

Olga said, 'No dough?'

Duffy nodded. 'That's right. No dough.'

She was silent for a minute. 'And then . . .?'

'Morgan's got big ideas. He thinks he's the only big shot round here. He told me to lay off the big dough with a few compliments on the side.'

Olga took her hands away and began to pull off her gloves. 'I expected it, didn't you?' she said. 'Does this dough mean anything to you?'

Duffy said, 'How do you mean, anything?'

'High-pressure bastards like Morgan can't imagine you're serious. You've got to have a reputation as a killer to get away with a proposition that you've put up.'

Duffy said, 'For God's sake, what can I do?'

She leant forward, touched the spring on the dashboard, and took out the Colt automatic. 'A rat less won't make any difference. Pop him, before he pops you.'

Duffy looked at the gun with distaste. He shook his head. 'No,' he said, 'I guess I wouldn't go that far.'

For a moment she sat very still, then she said, 'He's right. You're soft and you're yellow.'

Duffy took the gun from her and put it back into the panel. He sat looking at the knife-edge crease of his trousers. 'No dough's worth murder,' he said. 'If you and me are going to get along, we got to think the same way.'

She put her hand on his arm. 'I guess I'm a heel,' she said.

'Forget it,' he said. 'You're fine.'

'You go ahead. The next move's yours.'

'Let's take Gleason for a ride. If we get some dough out of him, we can scram to the coast. Would you like that? Some nice hot place with plenty of yellow sand. With a sky a real blue and just you and me?'

She leant back. 'It sounds pretty good.'

'It would be a lot better than having the cops chasing you and getting that nice little bottom of yours burnt. Come on, honey, let's look Gleason up.'

He started the engine and drove out of Central Park, down Second Avenue.

She said, 'Go along the river. It's nice there.'

He turned left when he could and came out at Bellevue Hospital. They drove with the traffic as far as the Williamsburg Bridge, then Duffy spun the wheel and they headed East.

They got back to his apartment just as the evening sun was dropping behind the roofs, throwing long, starved shadows.

They left the Buick at the kerb and walked up the stairs together. Duffy said, 'It seems a mighty long time since I had my last drink.'

'How about putting on the glad rags and taking me out?' she asked.

He put his hand on her back and pushed her a little. 'These stairs are hell, ain't they? Sure, we'll go places, but I want Gleason first.'

He opened the door of the apartment and they walked in together. Then Duffy said, 'Well . . .'

The room was a complete shambles. The furniture was overturned, drawers had been jerked out and left piled on the floor, the contents strewn over the carpet. The overstuffed furniture had been ripped to pieces and the stuffing dumped in piles. Pictures had been taken down from the walls and were lying with their backs cut. A tornado had certainly hit that room.

Duffy said gently, 'Gleason trying to save himself some dough.'

Olga wandered round the room, stepping carefully. 'That was a swell idea of yours about the bank.'

Duffy nodded. His face was hard and cold. 'I'll fix that smart bastard,' he said.

She said, 'There's time for that. You'd better move over to my place.'

He looked round the wreckage. 'I guess it don't really matter. We're due to pull out tomorrow, so what the hell.' He wandered into his bedroom and looked round with a grimace. The room had been searched as thoroughly as the sitting-room. There was a lot more mess, because the mattress and the pillows had been ripped.

Olga peered round the door. 'Our love-bed's been destroyed.'

'To hell with that,' Duffy said. 'They've stolen my whisky.' He dug about under the bed and dragged out two battered suitcases covered with feathers. 'Get going,' he said. 'Do some work for a change.'

Just then the telephone bell began to ring, and he went over to answer it, leaving her sorting his shirts and things from the wreckage.

It was Sam at the other end.

'Why, Sam,' Duffy was pleased. 'I'm glad you 'phoned.'

'Listen, you bum,' Sam sounded excited. 'Don't tell me you let that hot mamma go home to her people.'

Duffy said softly into the 'phone, 'She's in the other room.'

Sam groaned. 'That dame'll get you into trouble. Look, Bill, for God's sake chuck this thing, will you? I've heard the *Post* will give you a job, right up your street, and a swell equipment on the side.'

Duffy said, 'Thanks, pal, but I'm on to something big. Not peanut money, but the right stuff. I'm getting out tomorrow and I'm hitting the coast. When I've spent it all, I'll be back. Olga and me are getting on fine.'

Sam said, 'Alice'll kill me if I don't bring you back tonight. She told me to drag you by the short hairs.'

'It's time you left Alice, if that's the way she's talking.' Duffy grinned. 'No, I'm going ahead. When we're in the money, we'll invite you over.'

'It's on the level?' Sam sounded worried.

'Is any big dough on the level?' Duffy asked. 'Don't you sweat about me, I'm okay.'

Sam said, 'I'm going to have a sweet time with Alice tonight.'

'Tell her about Olga. She'll understand. Tell her Olga's swell. She won't expect me then.'

'Is she?' Sam sounded curious.

'Is she what?'

'Swell.'

'O boy! Listen, that honey's—' Duffy broke off as Olga walked into the room. 'Well, Sam, I'll be seeing you. Don't do anything you wouldn't like me to know about.' He dropped the receiver on to the prong.

Olga smiled at him. 'I heard. I'm glad.'

'You packed my things?'

'Just finished. There's so much junk.'

'Leave it. We ain't coming back.'

He put his arms round her. 'I like you a lot,' he said.

She pulled his face down to hers hungrily. 'Was I really good for you?' she whispered.

He said, 'Huh-uh.'

She put her mouth against his neck. 'Best of all?' she asked, taking a little of his skin between her teeth.

He pressed her to him and said, 'Sure, best of all.'

They stood there for a long time, just holding each other. Duffy liked the feel of her hair against his face. Then he pushed her away gently, holding her at arm's length. 'I wonder if we've been crazy, going for a gang like Morgan's,' he said. 'I could get a job right now, and we could settle down.'

'Play Gleason and we'll skip,' she said.

Duffy shrugged. He walked over to his bags and closed them, pulling the straps down hard. 'Yeah,' he said, 'you ain't Alice, are you?'

She looked puzzled. 'Alice?' she said. 'Who's Alice?'

Duffy grinned at her, but his mind was not with her.

'Oh, nothing – she's a sucker. Dough don't mean a thing to her. It's love in a poorhouse with her.'

Olga shrugged. 'That type's nearly dead,' she said a little scornfully, 'but you find 'em sometimes.'

Duffy stood looking round the room, holding the bags in either hand. He stood there so long that Olga touched his arm.

'Let's go, hophead,' she said.

Duffy said, 'Sure.' He walked to the door and then stopped again. 'I ain't ever going to see this joint again,' he said.

Olga pushed past him into the corridor. 'Who cares?' she asked, walking down the stairs.

Duffy looked after her, put one of the bags on the floor, shut the door, picked the bag up again, and followed her down.

CHAPTER ELEVEN

Back at Olga's villa, Duffy immediately put through a call to Annabel. While he was waiting for the connection, Olga began packing. Duffy could hear her moving about in the bedroom, overhead, singing in a husky monotone, but with plenty of swing with it.

The line connected with a little plop, and he said, 'Hullo.'

Annabel's breathless voice floated to his ear. 'Who is it?' she asked.

Duffy said, 'Your boy friend there? This is Duffy.'

'You're going to make a bad move soon,' she said fiercely, 'and I'm going to get a big laugh when you fall down.'

Duffy said, 'I ain't got time to talk to you just now, hot pants. Get Gleason.'

She said very evenly, 'They put smart guys like you in a gasoline bath and drop in a match.'

Gleason must have taken the 'phone from her. Duffy heard him say, 'Pipe down, for Gawd's sake.'

'Gleason?' Duffy asked.

'Yeah. You ready to play ball?'

'Sure, I'm ready to trade. Competition wasn't so hot. They offered forty grand, no more, no less. It's yours for fifty.'

Gleason raved, 'How the hell can I get fifty grand together?'

Duffy's mouth shaped into a smile, but his eyes were mirthless. 'I'm moving out tomorrow first thing,' he said. 'I don't care who has the list, but I want somebody's cash tonight. Fifty grand ain't all that big, for an outfit like yours.'

Gleason said, 'You're going to pay for this, you sonofabitch.'

Duffy said, 'Not until I get the dough and you get the book. After that, we'll all have to watch out.'

Gleason was silent for a moment. Then he said, 'I can't bring cash; I'll make it a certified cheque.'

'Cash,' Duffy's voice was hard. 'I'm feeding at the "Red Ribbon" tonight around eighty-thirty. If you ain't there by the time I'm through the deal's off. And it's gotta be cash.' He dropped the receiver back and went upstairs.

Olga was kneeling before a large cabin trunk. The floor was strewn with her clothes.

Duffy said, 'For God's sake . . .'

She turned her head and smiled at him. 'Come and help,' she said.

He looked at the small clock on the mantelshelf. From where he stood he could just make out the tiny hands. It was six-thirty. He put his hands under her elbows and brought her to her feet.

'Listen, baby,' he said patiently, 'this is going to be a quick journey. Leave all this junk. Just pack a bag. I'll buy you the world when we're out of this.'

She made a little face. 'They're so lovely.' She turned and looked at the things lying about.

'Come on,' he urged, 'time's moving.'

Together, they packed two large grips. Then Duffy went downstairs. He went into the kitchen and found a full bottle of Scotch. Taking two glasses, he went upstairs again. Putting the bottle on the small table by the bed he said, 'Let's have a drink.'

Olga came over and tore off the tissue wrapping round the bottle and flipped up the patent stopper. She splashed three inches of whisky into each glass.

Duffy said, 'To us,' and they drank. 'We're feeding at the "Red Ribbon" tonight.'

She added some ginger ale to the whisky.

'And then . . .?'

'Gleason might bring the dough. I think he will. If he does, we get in the Buick and get out of town quick.'

'And the lists?'

He nodded. 'Sure, I ain't forgotten them. I'm going to collect right now. I'll be gone about half an hour. You change. Put on something you can travel in.'

She came over to him and put her arms tightly round his neck.

'What's this?' he asked.

She raised herself on her toes and whispered urgently in his ear.

He looked at the clock, then he shook his head. 'Not now,' he said gently.

Her cool arms tightened, pulling his head down. 'Please . . .' she said, very low. 'Now.'

He put his lips gently on hers and pressed her to him, but his mind was elsewhere. He was thinking of Gleason, of Morgan, of the money, of how he was going to slip out of town. He was surprised at her. He thought this was a hell of a time to start a thing like this.

Then he put up his hands and took her arms from his neck, and pushed her away, still holding her arms.

'Tonight,' he said firmly. 'Look at the time. I've gotta get to the bank.'

A faint colour came to her face, and she didn't look at him. She turned away. 'The bank will be shut, won't it?' she said, still keeping her back to him. He noticed how toneless her voice was.

'Yeah, but I fixed that. There's an audit that's keeping 'em late. The teller there's a pal of mine. I warned him I might want the list late.'

He wandered over to her. 'You ain't sore with me?' he said gently, putting his arms round her.

She turned her head. She was still flushed. 'No. I'm not sore.' Then she said fiercely, 'If only it were all over. If only we were out of this with the money, and safe.'

Duffy said, 'Now don't go into a spin. It's going to work out okay, you see.'

'But you don't know,' she said, her breasts suddenly rising and falling. 'Bill, you don't know. I've been through so much . . . and – and now I've found you. I'm frightened it won't be all right.'

Duffy said, 'Hey! You don't want to get worked up. I tell you, we'll get away with it. We're going to have a fine time. We're going to be in the dough. You and me. We're going to have dough to burn . . . you see.'

She said quite quietly, 'I feel something horrible's going to happen.'

Duffy said, 'Skip it, honey. The Scotch's got hold of you.' He kissed her and he had to push her gently from him. Then he walked to the door. 'I shan't be long,' he said over his shoulder, and shut the door behind him.

She stood motionless where he had left her, then she suddenly said in a low voice, 'Come back, I'm scared. Bill, come back. . . .'

Out in the street, Duffy paused to light a cigarette. He threw the match from him and climbed into the Buick. As he started the engine he saw in his driving-mirror a big Packard turn into the street and drive slowly towards him. He glanced at it and then engaged his gear. His mind was still brooding on his future plans.

Pushing the pedal down, he drove the Buick fast. The Packard vanished from his mirror, and he thought no more about it.

At the bank there was a slight delay. Duffy had trouble in convincing the watchman that he had arranged to speak to the teller. The watchman was a stolid Irishman, with a big, beefy face, and not much brain.

Duffy took him through the explanation slowly again.

'Sure,' the watchman nodded his head, 'But this joint's closed, see?' He said the last word with obvious triumph.

Duffy said bleakly, 'Listen, punk, get going and tell Anscombe I'm here, or I'll get you fired.'

The watchman blinked at him, then thinking it wouldn't hurt him to inquire, he grumblingly left Duffy to cool his heels in the street. He came back again, after a delay that infuriated Duffy, and opened the iron-studded door.

'Come in,' he said shortly. 'This is mighty irregular.'

Duffy stepped in and stood waiting. A flustered clerk came over to him and Duffy nodded at him. 'I want that note-book I deposited,' he said shortly.

'Sure,' the clerk said. 'Mr. Anscombe's getting it for you.'

Anscombe came out of his office at the end of the hall and waved. He walked towards Duffy with a springy step. In his hand was the note-book.

'This is what you want, isn't it?' he said. 'I got it out as soon as the janitor brought me your name. Take it and give me a receipt. I'm doing you a favour. We oughtn't to do business as late as this.'

Duffy took the note-book, glanced at it, put it in his pocket and scribbled his name on the slip of paper Anscombe held out to him.

'Much obliged,' he said. 'I want this in a hurry, and it's worth something.'

Anscombe came with him to the door. He seemed in a hurry to get rid of him. Duffy stepped into the street. The air was very close. He cocked his eye at the sky. 'Looks like a storm,' he said.

Anscombe said it did; then he said good night, and shut the door. Duffy grinned a little, found that he was sweating, and blotted his face with his handkerchief. Then he walked over to the Buick and climbed in. He pressed the spring in the panel that held the guns, took one of the automatics out, glanced at the clip and shoved it down the waist of his trousers. He took out the note-book and put it in the panel. Then he pressed the spring and snapped it shut. It would be safe there, he thought.

The clock on the dashboard stood at seven twenty-five when he pulled up again at Olga's villa. He got out of the car and noticed that the light was still burning in her bedroom.

He said, 'I bet she's fretting over those dresses still.' He walked up the path, feeling the gravel through his thin soles. Then he opened the door with the key she had given him and entered the hall, shutting the door behind him.

He said, raising his voice, 'You dressed yet?' He didn't wait for her reply, but went into the sitting-room to get some cigarettes. He stopped at the doorway, feeling suddenly cold. Then he said, 'For God's sake . . .'

The room had been torn to pieces in the same way as his apartment had been. He just took one quick glance, then he blundered up the stairs, his legs curiously weak. At the top of the stairs he hesitated, then he called, 'Honey!' The sound of his voice quite startled him. It was hoarse and quavering.

'If those lugs have touched her,' he thought. He took a step forward, then stopped again. 'Honey,' he shouted. 'You there?'

The silence in the house mocked him. He put his hand on the gun butt and pulled the gun out. Then he began to slide forward silently, his feet making no sound on the carpet. He reached the bedroom door and put his hand on the knob. Then he gently turned the handle, holding the gun waist-high. He walked in.

Olga was lying on the floor, with a knife in her left breast. The knife had been driven in so hard that it had sealed the wound. She hadn't bled at all. The wrap she had put on just before Duffy had left had been torn from her, and was lying at the other end of the room, where it had been thrown. Her large eyes were open and her lips were parted, showing a little of her small white teeth. She didn't look scared, just surprised.

Duffy stood looking at her for a long time. The only sound in the room was the sharp busy ticking of the clock. Duffy didn't have to touch her to know she was dead.

For a moment the only thing that Duffy could think of was that she had offered herself to him not an hour ago, and he had refused.

A little trickle of sweat ran from under his hat, down his nose to his chin. He still stood looking at Olga. The telephone began to ring downstairs insistently. Duffy raised his head and listened. Then he turned and went down into the sitting-room. He pulled the telephone to him and said, 'Yes?'

The dry, brittle voice of the little guy said, 'We're waiting for that list. Zero hour's eleven o'clock. Then we come and get it.'

Duffy said through his teeth, 'Go and — yourself,' and hung up.

He climbed the stairs once more and went into the bedroom. He picked up the wrap from the floor and covered Olga with it. His hands shook when he touched her flesh. He said, 'I am sorry about this, honey,' just as if she could hear him, and he picked her up and carried her to the bed. Then he touched her hair very gently with his finger-tips, letting them move slowly down her face. 'You've had all the bad breaks, ain't you?' He stooped and kissed her full lips, feeling them growing cold against his. Then he stood up, examined his clothes for bloodstains, satisfied himself that there weren't any, and walked to the door.

'Take it easy, buddy,' a hard voice said.

Duffy raised his eyes. He felt no shock. Standing in the door was a cop, holding a gun in his hand. Just behind him, Duffy could see another flat cap.

Duffy said, 'I'm glad you've come. They've killed my girl friend.'

The first cop said, 'Keep your hands still.' The other cop came round and walked slowly towards Duffy, watching him carefully.

Duffy said, 'What's this?'

The first cop said, 'Frisk him. He'll have a rod.'

Duffy said, 'You're dead wrong.' He had left his gun on the settee, when he had carried Olga to the bed. It was lying there, half hidden by a cushion.

The second cop stepped round him cautiously, just as if he were a wild animal that might snap any time. When he got behind him, he ran his hands down Duffy's clothing, patting firmly. Then he stood back and shook his head. 'He ain't carryin' one,' he said.

Duffy said, 'Listen, you're wasting time.'

'Just a minute,' the first cop said, 'you're Duffy, ain't that right?'

Duffy said, 'Sure.'

They both looked at him as if surprised that he admitted it. Then the second cop wandered over to the bed and had a look at Olga. He pulled off the wrapper and gaped at her.

Duffy said savagely, 'Cover her up, you heel.'

The second cop jerked round. 'Keep your trap shut, punk,' he snarled. 'Another crack like that and I'll smack you down.'

The first cop said, glancing at the bed, 'She dead?'

'Yeah, this guy used a knife.'

Duffy said, 'I came back and found her like that.'

'You hear that? He came back and found her like that!' The first cop grinned. 'You're coming with us . . . come on.'

'You ain't charging me with killing her?' Duffy was incredulous.

'Get wise to yourself.' The first cop liked the sound of his voice. 'We've been tipped off.'

Duffy felt a restricting band across his chest. 'I don't get that,' he said slowly.

'That dame had a hidden roll salted away in this joint, and you knew it. You made up to her and tried to get the roll away, but it didn't work. So you rubbed her out, and took the joint to pieces. The roll is on you, now, ain't that right, Gus?'

The second cop nodded. He walked over to Duffy and put his hand in Duffy's inside pocket. He pulled out a flat packet of currency.

Duffy said, very evenly, 'A frame-up, huh?'

Gus looked at him and grinned. 'Between you and me, you're right. You're bucking the wrong outfit, mug,' he said.

Duffy said, 'You ain't making this stick.'

The first copper shrugged. 'You don't know the half of it. You're going for a little ride right now.'

'There's a bottle of Scotch somewhere,' Duffy said, looking round the room. 'Mind if I cut the phlegm?'

Gus passed the end of a thick finger round the inside of his collar. 'We'll cut it, too.'

Duffy walked across the room, conscious of the hard unwavering watchfulness of the cop with the gun. His brain was ice-cold. If they were ready to frame him by such a clumsy method of palming money and planting it on him, they might even knock him off resisting arrest.

He picked up the whisky and filled the two glasses that Olga and he had used, half full.

As he turned, he intercepted a quick glance between the two cops. He felt himself go very cold. It told him what he suspected. He gave Gus one of the glasses and then wandered over to the other. 'I guess I can use the bottle,' he said carelessly.

The gun looked as big as a cannon trained on his vest, but he showed no sign of jumping nerves as he held out the glass. He was just about five feet away from the cop. Then he moved with incredible rapidity. He stepped quickly aside. At the same time he tossed the whisky into the cop's face.

The cop gave a howl, clapped one of his hands to his eyes, stepped back, and blindly pulled the trigger. The gun crashed. Duffy jumped in, threw himself on the cop's gun arm, and jerked the gun out of his hand.

The next sound he was conscious of was the breaking of glass. The cop was behaving like a madman, trying to get the whisky out of his eyes. Duffy had no time. He hit the cop, holding the gun by the barrel, between the eyes. Then he whirled round, expecting to run into a blast from the other cop.

Gus was standing with his hands on his belly, staring at his highly polished boots. Duffy saw blood oozing between his fingers. Gus fell on his knees, hesitated, his body swaying. Then he straightened out on his face.

Duffy said, 'I hope you liked it.' He went quickly to the luggage that was piled on the floor, selected a long strap from one of the grips, and bound the first cop's arms tightly. Then he went over to Olga, picked up the wrap, and covered her with it.

He moved silently and swiftly. All the time at the back of his brain he could see the jam he was in. He went back to the cop who was coming round. Duffy hauled him on to the settee, retrieved his gun from under the cushion, and stuck it down his waist-band. Then he slapped the cop across the face twice with his open hand.

The cop opened his eyes, gave a grunt, and then tried to sit up. Duffy said, 'Who's behind this frame-up?'

The cop glared, but didn't say anything.

Duffy drew his gun and put it close to the cop's face. 'I'm in a hurry,' he said, his eyes like chips of ice. 'Spill it quick, or I'll hook your eyes out with this gun-sight.'

The cop suddenly went limp and began to sweat. He mumbled, 'Miss English tipped us off. She gave us a nice slice to knock you, resisting arrest. We've worked for her before.'

Duffy said, 'Her father in this racket?'

The cop shook his head. 'He don't know nothing.'

Duffy went over to Gus, turned him over with his foot, searched in his pockets, and found the roll of notes. He counted them carefully. Then he looked up. 'There's ten grand here,' he said. 'Was that your cut?'

The cop shook his head. 'That was evidence against you,' he said. 'That dame sure wants you out of the way.'

In the street, Duffy heard a car draw up. He ran to the window in time to see four uniformed police officers tumbling out. Two quick steps took him to the door. Then he slid down the flight of stairs, darted into the kitchen as the front door burst open. Quietly, he let himself out the back door. He could hear the cop upstairs yelling his head off. He told himself that he'd got to make the Buick. He ran round the small garden, paused when he reached the front, and peered carefully round the corner of the house. He could see the police car, and a little way further on was the Buick. He ran hard, not caring how much noise he made. As he reached the Buick and pulled open the heavy door he heard a shout; but he didn't stop. He scrambled into the car, swearing softly and continuously. The cold sweat ran down his face, and he expected to feel the jagged pain of a hot slug smash into him. As he slammed the door to, a gun roared from the bedroom window.

He started the engine, revved hard, engaged his gear, and shot the Buick down the road. He heard three distinct thuds on the back of the car before he jerked round the corner.

He said, 'It's going to be a grand finish.' And his face stiffened into a hard mask as he swung the quivering car to the bends.

CHAPTER TWELVE

Ross was having a snack when Duffy drove in. He waddled out of the office, his little mouth tight with food. He nodded at Duffy, gulped, then said, 'Anything wrong?'

Ross always expected trouble. Duffy got out of the car and said, 'The wagon's hot. Gimme new plates.'

For his size, Ross moved amazingly quickly. He went back to the office, and returned with a new set of plates. Duffy helped him change them. Ross said, 'You jammed?'

'Listen, pal, ask nothing and hear nothing. I'm buying this box. Maybe, you won't see me any more.'

Ross raised his eyebrows and put his hands on his enormous buttocks. 'Okay,' he said, 'keep her, you've looked after me before now.'

Duffy took out the roll of notes and peeled some off. He stuck them in Ross's belt. 'Buy yourself a yacht with that,' he said. Then he climbed back in the car. Ross put his head through the window. 'If you want a good hide-out,' he said 'go to the Bronx on Maddiston and tell Gilroy I sent you.'

Duffy repeated, 'Bronx on Maddiston.'

Ross took his head from the window, glanced out into the street. 'It's clear,' he said, 'I'm sorry about this.'

Duffy showed his teeth. 'Me too,' he said. 'Others are going to share our grief.'

He raised his hand in a salute, then rolled the Buick into the street again. He drove carefully up Lafayette Street, cut across Broadway to Washington Square and headed for Greenwich Village. He parked outside a drug store and went in.

Several men were eating at the quick-lunch bar, and Duffy sat on an empty stool. He had a chicken sandwich. He washed it down with three quick drags from the pint flask he had taken from the car. The whisky was rough, but there was plenty of life in it. When he had finished the sandwich, he crossed over to the telephone booths and shut himself in. He dialled the *Tribune* number and asked for Sam. When Sam came to the 'phone, Duffy said, 'Sam? Got any news?'

Sam said in a low voice, 'I gotta see you.'

Duffy said, 'Can you come out to Dinty's? I'll go straight there.'

Sam said, 'Yeah,' and hung up.

Duffy walked out of the drug store, looked up and down the street before he crossed the pavement, then climbed into the Buick. He let in his clutch and drove over to Dinty's. He parked the car in the underground garage, took the lift to the top floor, asked for a private room.

The waiter who served him said, 'A lady is coming?'

Duffy shook his head. 'Get the room ready, have some rum, absinthe and dressing up there, and some Club sandwiches. I'm waiting downstairs for a friend.'

Sam came in the hall a little while after. They went up together in the lift. Neither of them said anything, but Sam kept wiping off his hands and face with a large handkerchief. They went into the room and Duffy shut the door.

Sam said, 'You gone crazy?'

Duffy went over to the table and began to fix the drinks. 'Has it broken yet?' he asked.

'They're printing it now. I was down at the station when the report came in.' Sam was trying to be casual, but he was as jittery as a hophead.

Duffy poured the drinks from the shaker, and silently pushed one of the glasses over.

Sam said, 'You're in a hell of a spot.'

'Annabel's playing this,' Duffy said savagely. 'She's pulling strings behind the scene.'

'What happened, for God's sake?'

Duffy drained his glass, and immediately filled up again. 'We were set to pull out. I went down to the bank to get the book out. When I got back, I found the joint in pieces and Olga dead. Some rat had stuck a knife in her. I must have been crazy. Instead of grabbing the 'phone and reporting it right away, I ran round in circles. Then a couple of cops moved in. They had the story pat. I'd killed Olga for her roll. They even found the dough on me. One of 'em palmed it, put his hand in my pocket and seemed surprised to find it clinging to his hand.'

Sam stared. 'Why the frame? They had you sewed up tight enough without that.'

Duffy shrugged. 'You telling me? The sweet part of the set-up was they intended to iron me out. I could see them getting set for it. Resisting arrest, closing the case, and slapping the murder rap on a corpse. Save the State plenty. It was nice planning, but they were slow on it. One cop shot the other, and I ducked out as the patrol wagon arrived.'

Sam fidgeted with his glass. 'You're it,' he said.

'Annabel knocked her off.' Duffy sat on the edge of the table, he held his glass a little on one side, so that the liquor slopped slightly on the carpet. 'They thought they'd get the list without paying. Well, they won't. It's going to be just too bad for them.'

'You better skip while the goin's good. You can't stand up against this outfit. It's too big for you.'

Duffy said evenly, 'I'm finishing this. They've had all the fun up to now. Olga said I'd never get anywhere with those rats till I took a gun, and by God, she's right.'

Sam said, 'You liked that Jane, didn't you?'

Duffy's mouth set in a thin line. He kept his eyes on the floor. 'I was getting used to her,' he said at last. 'She had all the bad breaks.'

'I still say skip. You can't buck the cops, as well as Morgan. They're too big for you.'

Duffy said, 'You keep out of this, Sam. I'm going out to the

Bronx on Maddiston. Ross's got a hide-out there. If things begin to break wrong, you can find me there. I'll wait until the heat cools off, then I'll start something.'

Sam said, 'I got to go. I'm on my way to the Villa. All the boys are down there.'

Duffy went over to him. 'Tell Alice to keep her pants on. I guess this's bound to happen sometime. I wasn't cut out for a soft life.'

Sam moved to the door. 'If you want some jack, I can stake you.'

Duffy grinned. 'You'd be surprised just how much dough's coming my way.'

They didn't shake hands, they just looked at each other. Sam gave a worried smile, it hadn't much heart in it, but he smiled. Duffy nodded. 'You'll hear from me,' he said.

He waited until Sam had gone downstairs, poured himself another drink, lit a cigarette, then went out and down to the Buick.

Rain was beginning to fall in heavy drops. Duffy leant over and rolled up the off-side window, then he drove the Buick on to the street. As he threaded his way through the traffic, the rain drummed hard on the car roof. It was splashing knee-high off the pavement.

Duffy drove carefully. It took him quite a time to get to the Bronx, which was a basement club, with a convenient garage over the way. Duffy left the Buick at the garage and walked down into the club.

'Gilroy around?' he asked.

The thin man who opened the door looked at him suspiciously, said, 'Who wants him?'

'Tell him a friend of Ross.'

The thin man pulled the door open. 'Come in,' he said. When Duffy stepped into the dimly-lit passage, the thin man ran his hands down Duffy's suit. He stepped back. 'You can't bring a rod in here,' he said.

'Tell Gilroy,' Duffy snapped, 'and shut up.'

The thin man looked at him, hesitated, then walked down the passage. He disappeared through a dirty green baize door, and Duffy leant against the wall, waiting. After a short delay

the door opened again and a very light-coloured negro came
out. He was tall and slender, with a heavy wave in his oily hair.
He gave Duffy a hard look. 'You want me?'

Duffy said, 'Ross sent me here. I want to keep under cover
for a few days.'

Gilroy passed a long thin hand over his hair. 'Okay,' he said.
'A hundred bucks a day.'

Duffy sidled close. 'Forget it,' he said. 'You don't make
profit out of me.'

Gilroy looked at him, then his large lips smiled. 'No,' he
said, 'that was bad. Ross's a good friend of mine. Make it
twenty-five.'

Duffy took out his roll, peeled ten saw bucks and handed
them over. 'That'll hold you for a few days,' he said.

Gilroy moved near the light, counted the bills, put them in
his pocket, and grinned some more.

He said, 'How low do you want to stay, mister?'

'When you read the papers, you'll see,' Duffy told him. 'I
want a meal, plenty to drink and a telephone.'

Gilroy led him through the baize door, down three stairs,
past a bead-curtained door and through another door at the end
of a dimly-lit passage. The room was small. It contained a bed,
table, two arm-chairs, and a small radio.

'I'll get you some chuck right away.'

Duffy said, 'How safe's this joint?'

Gilroy rolled his eyes. 'It's okay. I'm paying plenty for protection. The bulls won't worry you here.'

He left Duffy and shut the door behind him. In the corner of
the room, standing on a small table, was a telephone. Duffy
looked at it, his mouth pursed thoughtfully. Then he walked
over and dialled.

He recognized Gleason's voice. 'Too bad you didn't get the
list when you knocked my girl-friend off,' he said, biting off
each word.

There was a startled gasp as Gleason caught his breath.
'Why, you double-crossing rat,' he jerked out. 'What's the big
idea? I'm just back from the "Red Ribbon". I had the dough
and you never showed up.'

Duffy said, 'Cut the comedy. You killed Olga and you

pinned it on me. Okay, wise guy, you ain't getting away with it . . .'

Gleason broke in. 'What the hell is this? Who's Olga?'

Duffy stared at the wall for a full minute, then he said, 'I'm coming over. You got that dough still?'

Gleason said, 'Sure.'

And Duffy hung up.

Gilroy walked in with a bottle of whisky, three bottles of ginger ale and a glass. 'Your chuck's coming right now.'

Duffy took the whisky from him and poured out a long shot. He shook his head at the ginger ale, and drank quickly. Just then a knock came on the door, and the thin man came in carrying a tray. He put it on the table, and glanced at Duffy before going out.

Duffy sat down and began to eat. Gilroy hung around, fidgeting by the radio. He said at last, 'I knew that dame.'

Duffy looked up, a fork full of food suspended before his mouth. 'Huh?'

Gilroy said, 'I guess you'd better get moving.'

Duffy laid the fork down. 'What the hell's this?'

'Olga Shann, I knew her.'

Duffy picked up the fork again. 'She was a swell kid,' he said. 'I didn't kill her, if that's what's biting you.'

Gilroy stirred restlessly, beads of sweat hung on his top lip. 'It looks that way,' his voice was exceedingly hostile.

Duffy went on eating. 'A little judy called Annabel English shoved that knife into her,' he said. 'This is a frame-up. I'm it.'

Gilroy took out a handkerchief and carefully wiped his mouth. He stood still, looking at his bright yellow shoes.

Duffy finished the meal in silence. Then he drank some more whisky and sat back. He lit a cigarette, and forced two thin jets of smoke down his nostrils. 'If you like that dame as much as I did,' he said, 'I know how you feel.'

Gilroy relaxed a little and came over to the table. 'Ross's never sent me a bum yet,' he said. 'I guess I was wrong.'

Duffy nodded. 'Sure, that's okay.'

'I'd like to make this a personal matter.' Gilroy studied his pinkish nails. 'If you want any help, I've a nice little outfit.'

Duffy grinned. 'I've gotta see this through myself.'

'Sure, sure,' Gilroy nodded his head. 'Still, you can't always beat the rap.'

Getting to his feet, Duffy said, 'I'll file that offer away. I might have to use it.'

He moved to the door, then looked over his shoulder. 'It's on the street now?'

Gilroy nodded. 'Yeah, the heat's on good.'

A hard little smile came to Duffy's lips. 'I ain't starting anything just yet,' he said. 'I'll be back some time.'

He went over to the garage, got into the Buick and drove over to Annabel's apartment. He parked up a side street and walked back. At the entrance to the organ loft, he paused. At the corner he could see a flat cap, standing under a street light. He turned quickly and walked once more back to the Buick. He got in and sat there, watching the cop. The rain had ceased, but the pavements were still wet and shiny in the street lights. The cop moved on after a bit, and Duffy went back to the entrance. He opened the door with the key he still had with him, and silently went up the stairs.

When he got into the loft, he saw Gleason sitting in the room below nursing an automatic. Sinking on his knee, so that his head did not appear over the balcony, he watched Gleason for several minutes. Then he said in a hard voice, 'Put your rod on the floor, or you'll get it.'

Gleason started, hastily put the gun at his feet, and looked up.

Duffy stood up and leant over the rail. He kept the Colt steady. 'Where's Annabel?' he asked.

Gleason said in a dry, strangled voice, 'She ain't in.'

Duffy swung his legs over the balcony and sat there. 'I'm coming down,' he said. 'Don't start anything. I'm itching to blast you.'

He pushed himself off, breaking his fall with one hand. Gleason's face was a little drawn. He kept both hands folded in his lap.

Duffy walked over and sat on the edge of the table. He held the Colt down by his side. He reached out a foot and kicked Gleason's gun under a chair, away from Gleason. He said, 'I gotta lot to talk to you about.'

Gleason looked at him, twitched his mouth a little, but said nothing.

Duffy said, 'You've double-crossed me once. You've pulled a fast one at my joint, and another at the Villa. You tried to slap a murder rap on me. Well, you've had fun. Now I'm going to have some.'

Gleason said in a thin voice, 'I don't know what you're talking about.'

His face was so blank that Duffy stopped talking and stared at him. 'Okay, you don't know anything about it,' he said. 'What *do* you know?'

'I'm dealing it off the top deck,' Gleason said. 'I want the book, you got it, and I'm paying for it. I went to the "Red Ribbon" with the dough as arranged, but you didn't show up. I came back here and you 'phoned. That's all.'

Duffy rubbed the short hairs on his nape with the flat of his hand. Then he said, 'Who killed Weidmer?'

Gleason shifted his eyes. 'That doesn't get you anywhere.'

'You're wrong. Who killed him? Come on! If you know you'll let yourself out of this.'

Gleason said, 'But, I don't know.'

Duffy raised the Colt. 'This is my first killing.' He spoke very harshly. His face had gone oyster colour. Two thin lines ran down the sides of his mouth. 'I hope I do it right.'

Gleason's skin went a little yellow, and he opened his eyes very wide. He said, running all his words together, 'It was that damned little judy.'

Duffy pushed his hat to the back of his head. His face glistened in the diffused light. 'You damned louse,' he said, 'you nearly made me kill you.'

Gleason lay back in the chair. He looked bad.

Duffy said, 'What's this dame to you?'

'She's my wife.' Gleason put his hands on his coat lapels to stop them from shaking. 'I wish to God I'd never seen her.'

'So that's it, is it? She killed Cattley and Weidmer and Olga?'

Gleason shifted. 'Who's this Olga you keep bringing up?'

'Never mind.' Duffy got to his feet. 'You ought to watch that dame, she's dangerous.'

Gleason tried to cross his legs, but couldn't quite make it. He stared down at the carpet. 'She's hop screwy,' he said. 'I can't shake her. She'd stick a knife into me.'

'How much jack have you got?'

Gleason looked up sharply. 'You said fifty grand. I got twenty-five here.' He took a long sealed envelope from his inside pocket and laid it on the table.

Duffy looked at the seal, then he said, 'Open it.'

Gleason tried twice, but his fingers bothered him. Duffy leant over, took the envelope from him, put his gun down on the table, and tore off the end of the envelope. He shook the contents on to the table and looked at it. Then he picked up the thin sheaf of notes and put it in his pocket. He took the note-book out and tossed it into Gleason's lap.

Gleason looked at him in complete astonishment. Duffy shook his head. 'You expected a double-cross, ain't that right? I guess you ain't keeping it long.'

Gleason thumbed through the book as if he couldn't believe his eyes. Duffy went over and picked up Gleason's gun, took out the clip and then tossed the gun back on the floor. He put his own Colt down his waist-band and adjusted the points of his vest.

Gleason looked up at him. 'This is the first level deal that's happened to me,' he said.

Duffy's eyes were still hard. 'You don't know a thing. You ain't going to keep that list long. Morgan's after it.'

Gleason stiffened and got to his feet. 'Morgan? How the hell did Morgan know?'

Duffy shrugged. 'I guess I talked too much,' he said. 'Anyway, that's your funeral.'

He walked to the door. 'I gotta few things to fix, then I'm blowing.'

Gleason stood in the middle of the room, the note-book in his hands, staring at the floor. Duffy took one look at him, shrugged, and opened the door. *Annabel was standing there pointing a .38 at his belly.*

Duffy raised his hands just above his waist very quickly. She said, 'Reach up, punk, the roof's not high enough.'

Gleason came across quickly and jerked Duffy's gun out. Then he said in a low voice, 'Walk backwards.'

Duffy obeyed. Annabel came into the light. Her face was very pale, and it had a scraped, bony look. She looked a hundred years old, standing there hating him with her eyes. Gleason put Duffy's gun into his hip pocket and then went across to Duffy and took the sheaf of notes from him. He gave a little grin. 'Too bad,' he said.

Duffy continued to look at Annabel. He said very evenly and through his teeth, 'You'd better let that heat off. I'll kill you if I get the chance.'

She said, 'Sit down.'

Duffy sat down because he wanted to, not because she told him to. She said to Gleason, 'Put the radio on.'

Gleason looked at her, puzzled, then walked over to the radio, that was a little to the right and behind Duffy. When Gleason turned his back, Duffy saw Annabel stiffen. Her eyes seemed to film over, and her lips came off her teeth. Not understanding, he stared at her, then he suddenly guessed and gave a shout. Annabel shot at Gleason twice. The gun barked, then barked again. Gleason swung round, his face twisted, his eyes startled, unbelieving, frightened, then he crashed over, taking the radio with him.

'Don't move,' Annabel said to Duffy, swinging the gun round to him.

Duffy sat very still, looking at Gleason. Then he said through stiff lips, 'You poor devil.'

Annabel said, 'I've been waiting a chance to get rid of that punk for some time.' She spat each word at him.

'They'll burn you for this,' Duffy said coldly.

'Think so?' she laughed. 'Can't you see? Watch me pin it on you.'

She went over to Gleason's gun, lying on the floor, and picked it up. Then she backed away from Duffy. 'I'd like a chance of shooting you,' she said. 'So start something if you're tired of life.'

She wiped the .38 carefully on her skirt, then she tossed the gun beside Gleason. 'That's your gun,' she said, covering him with Gleason's automatic.

Duffy grinned. 'So what?'

She said, 'Don't you get it? I'm going to shoot you now. The police will find you. I shot you in self-defence after you killed Gleason. Don't you think I'm cute?'

Duffy got slowly out of his chair. 'You're nutty,' he said evenly, and began to walk towards her.

She waited until he was within two yards of her, then she pulled the trigger. Her lips were off her teeth and little white specks of foam touched her mouth. The automatic went click – click – click. Then Duffy put his hand on the automatic and jerked it out of her hand. 'I took the clip out before you showed up,' he said quietly, then he smacked her across her face with his open palm as hard as he could hit her. She bounced against the wall, slid down, and rolled on her side. She began to scream in a thin reedy tone that sent hot wires into Duffy's brain.

From the organ loft, a tight voice said, 'Pipe down, he ain't hurt you. It was just a slap.'

CHAPTER THIRTEEN

The little guy said, 'How the hell does one get down from this nest?'

Duffy looked at him, then he looked at Clive, and then he looked at Joe. Clive and Joe were carelessly holding guns. Duffy said, 'You jump.' He went over to the sideboard and began to pour himself a drink.

Annabel sat up, pressed herself against the wall, and stared up at the three in the loft.

The little guy swung his short legs over the balcony and let himself drop. He landed on his shoulders with a thud. He sat up carefully and cursed. Then he said, 'You come down, Clive; but Joe, you watch these birds and pop 'em if they get tough. You heard that, didn't you, Joe? I said pop 'em if they get tough.'

Joe leant over the balcony and looked down. He looked a little tired. 'Yeah,' he said, 'I heard you. I'm watching okay.'

Clive scrambled over the balcony, making black marks with the toes of his shoes on the wall.

Duffy drank a little of the Scotch and felt better. He said, 'You ain't met these two before, have you?' to the little guy. 'The stiff over there was Murray Gleason, and the red-head sitting on the floor showing all she's got is Annabel.'

The little guy giggled, then said, 'My, my, you go places, don't you?'

Duffy said, 'Sure. Well, now you're here, what's next?'

Clive went over to Gleason, turned him over, and searched him. He found the sheaf of notes and the little pocket-book. He came over with them to the little guy. They both examined the note-book carefully.

Duffy lost interest in them, he went over to Annabel. He said very quietly, 'When you killed Olga you started something. I'm going to pin that on to you, if it takes me a hundred years.'

She drew back her lips and spat at him. He raised his hand, looked at her, then stepped away. 'It's time you were dead,' he said.

The little guy held the note-book and said to Clive, 'Would you like to watch this?'

Clive said he would.

'Give him a hoop as well,' Duffy said.

The little guy looked at him with disapproval. 'I told you before not to make fun of him.'

Clive said, 'I'm going to rub this heel out.'

The little guy scratched his head, then looked up at Joe. 'You heard that?'

Joe grinned. 'Why not? It's some time since Clive knocked anyone off.'

The little guy said, 'Yes, that's right. It *is* some time. Yeah, okay, you knock him off.'

Clive turned slowly on Duffy, who was standing near the wall. Duffy's face was tense, he pushed out his chin a little, the muscles in his neck suddenly going hard.

Annabel said from the floor, 'Give it to him low down.'

Clive and the little guy both jerked their heads in her direction, and Duffy snapped up the light switch, then he dropped to his knees and shot away to the left. In his mind he could clearly see the wires that fed the two standard lamps. He groped for them, found nothing, groped again, touched them, and then pulled sharply. He felt them come away loose.

The little guy said in a sharp voice, 'Don't start shooting. We don't want the cops here. Clive, stand by the door. I'll put on the lights.'

Duffy grinned. He stood up, listening for the slightest sound. The darkness made him feel like a man.

Joe said, 'I'm coming down.'

The little guy said, 'Wait; I'll tell you.'

Duffy moved softly towards the little guy. When he got near enough as he could judge, he stopped. Quite close to him, he heard a rattle of matches. He balanced himself, and as the match flared up he hit the little guy right in the middle of his face. The match fell on the carpet and went out. Duffy took three quick steps away from the little guy, who was lying on the ground, collided with a chair. Joe fired just once. It was close enough. Duffy felt the bullet against his sleeve as it passed.

Moving to the door, he ran up against Clive. Clive gave a high scream, but Duffy's questing hands found his head, and he banged it back against the wall hard. Clive went limp.

The little guy said in a sudden panic, 'Quick, Joe! He's got Clive.'

Joe said, 'What the hell do you think I can do? I can't see.'

Holding Clive by the shirt-front, Duffy jerked the door open, and stepped into the hall, dragging Clive with him. The hall was in darkness. Duffy threw Clive on the floor, sprang back to the door, found the key on the outside, and turned it. Then he struck a match and flicked on the electric light switch.

Clive was lying in a heap, dazed. He stared up at Duffy with unseeing eyes. Duffy searched his pockets, found the notes and the little book and transferred them to his pocket, then he stood up.

'I guess I owe you something,' he said softly, and put his heel on Clive's upturned face, pressed down hard, turning the heel slowly. Clive clawed at his foot, and began to scream. Duffy said, 'Here it is, Nance, it's been coming to you for a long time.' He put his entire weight on his right leg and twisted his heel sharply. There was a cracking sound, and under his heel it felt soft. Clive stopped screaming. Duffy stepped away, dragged his heel once, then twice on the soft carpet, leaving two long smears of red. He opened the front door and stepped into the passage, and ran downstairs, not waiting for the elevator. Faintly, he could hear the thudding of Joe's shoulder against the locked door.

He reached the street. It was raining again. The air was heavy and very warm. He ran on to the Buick, pulled open the door and got in. Then he drove away very quickly.

The streets were less congested. He took half the time in getting back to the Bronx. Leaving the car in the garage, he walked down the steps of the basement and rapped on the door.

Gilroy opened it. The negro showed his big white teeth. 'You okay?' he asked.

Duffy nodded. He said, 'Come and have a drink.'

Gilroy followed him down the passage into the little room. Duffy sat on the bed and pushed his hat to the back of his head. Gilroy fixed the drinks, came over and gave Duffy a glass. He stood waiting. His thin face sleepy, but interested.

Duffy looked him over thoughtfully from the bed, scratched the side of his face, making a little rasping noise. Then he said, 'Perhaps you might like to come in on this.'

Gilroy lifted his shoulders. 'Maybe,' he said, 'it's nothing to me now.'

'Gleason was knocked off tonight,' Duffy said, swirling the whisky in the glass. 'I was there, so was Morgan's gang and Gleason's wife. She popped him and tried to pin it on me.'

Gilroy rolled up his eyes. 'They're slapping it on you all right,' he said at last.

Duffy nodded. 'Sure, they got a reason. I'm holding up a million-dollar racket.' He took the note-book out of his pocket and tossed it on the table. Gilroy picked it up curiously and examined it. Duffy could see it meant nothing to him.

He explained.

Gilroy sat listening, his black eyes half closed. He pursed his lips together. He said, at last, 'You gotta be careful.'

Duffy said, 'I know that.' He got to his feet and wandered round the small room. 'If Olga were here, I'd pull out, but where the hell can I go now?'

Gilroy thumbed the book over. 'You wouldn't get far,' he said.

Duffy shrugged. 'I don't know,' he said. 'I might.'

'You thinking of playing this further?'

Duffy stopped walking and stood very still. He looked hard at Gilroy. 'That depends a lot on you.'

Gilroy said, 'Where do I come in?'

'A while back, you offered me your outfit; I guess I can use it.'

Gilroy smoothed down his crinkly hair with his hand. 'How?' he said. He was being very cautious.

Duffy leant forward and tapped the top of the table with his index finger. 'I'd like to run Morgan out of town.'

Gilroy drew his breath in with a little hiss. 'You're nuts,' he said. 'You gotta have dough for a job like that.'

Duffy took from his pocket the thin sheaf of notes and put it on the table. Then from his side coat pocket he took the ten grand he had lifted off Gus, and laid it on top of the other money. Gilroy watched him fascinated.

'Thirty-five grand enough?' Duffy asked.

Gilroy eased his collar with a thin black finger. 'It helps,' he said slowly. 'Where the hell did that come from?'

Duffy scooped up the money and put it back in his pocket. 'It fell in my lap,' he said. 'What say? You on?'

Gilroy sat down, poured out more drinks and lit a cigarette. 'Let's talk about it. What's your idea?'

Duffy came over and sat down too. 'I don't know,' he said. 'I just want to run this Morgan louse out, and his gang with him.'

Gilroy screwed up his eyes, then said, 'Why?'

Duffy's mouth set. 'He thinks I can't do it. He's told me so. Well, I'm going to show the palooka he's bucking the wrong horse.'

Gilroy nodded. 'That's the way it goes, is it?'

Duffy said, 'Yeah, that's it.'

'You won't get far with the cops after you.'

'I've got that on the line. First thing tomorrow I'm getting protection.'

'Protection? Where do you get that from?'

'English.' Duffy leant back in the chair and took a long pull at his glass. 'I'm blowing the whole works to that guy, and then watch him cover me up.'

Gilroy said, 'You've got something there.'

Duffy said, 'Sure, I have. Once I get protection, I'm a big shot. I can handle Morgan with protection and an outfit like yours.'

Gilroy said, 'There's me, there's Shep, and there's Schultz.'

'Okay. Suppose we all get together, after I've seen English.'

Gilroy nodded and stood up. 'The boys get in around about one o'clock. If you can make it, we'll be here then.'

He wandered to the door. 'It ain't going to be easy,' he said.

Duffy was watching him cross the room. 'You ain't gone into it,' he said. 'It's a cinch.'

Gilroy nodded and went out, pulling the door behind him. Duffy got up and took off his coat. A knock came on the door and the thin man put his head round. 'There's a jane asking for you,' he said.

Duffy said, 'Sure, and I suppose you told her I was right inside?'

The thin man said, 'I told her I'd never heard of you, but it won't shift her. She says, "Tell him it's Alice", like that. So I come back, and here I am.'

'Well, for God's sake!' Duffy put on his coat. 'Shoot her in quick.'

The thin man shrugged and went away. He came back with Alice at his heels. Duffy went over to her and took her hands. He said, 'Why, honey . . .' then he stopped.

'Sam told me,' she said breathlessly. 'I had to see you. What is all this, Bill? The papers say you killed that woman. It's all in headlines.'

Duffy patted her arm. 'Swell of you to come,' he said, leading her over to the bed. 'Sit down, baby. Take the weight off your feet.'

'What are you going to do?' she said. 'Sam won't tell me anything.'

Duffy grinned. 'He's told you too much as it is,' he said. 'Listen, I didn't kill Olga. It was a frame-up. Look baby, I've got dough.' He took the money from his pocket and tossed it in her lap.

She gave a little shiver and put her hands behind her. She just sat and stared at the money. 'Take it away,' she said quickly.

Duffy stared at her. 'Look,' he urged, 'There's thirty-five grand there. Did you ever see so much dough all at once?'

She said again in a tone that was just off-pitch, 'Take it away.'

He picked up the money, a sulky look in his eyes. 'If that's the way you feel,' he said.

She put her hand on his arm. 'Oh, Bill, you're heading for trouble. Can't you see? For your own sake, please, stop it.'

Duffy put the money carefully in his side pocket. 'Now listen—' he began.

She interrupted him. 'Money isn't everything. You know it isn't. Please Bill, give yourself up. I know it'll be all right. We'll get someone to help you . . . get back to your job. Don't go on with this business.'

Duffy raised his hand. She took one look at the hard glint in his eyes, and she sat away from him and began to cry. Duffy said, 'I'm going through with this. I've been a little shot for years. I've been "Come here, you bastard", "Do this, you heel", "Get that, you punk" all my goddam life. I'm through with it now. I'm bucking an outfit that's supposed to be tough. Okay, I'm bucking 'em. I'm going to get an outfit twice as tough. Do you get that? Twice as tough! When I've got it, I'm going to be the big shot around here from now on. How do you like that?'

Alice got to her feet. She said in an unsteady voice, 'For God's sake, keep Sam out of this.'

Duffy said, 'I'm sorry, honey.' He felt a sudden tenderness for her. 'I'm just shooting off my mouth. I'm just wild. A no-good out of work. Forget it, will you?'

She looked at him for several seconds. 'You're going through with this, I know,' she said. 'You're going to hurt people and you're going to get hurt. Just to satisfy a little pride, a little ego in you. I can't stop you. When you're tired of this, come and see us. But stay away until you've got it out of your system. I've loved you a lot in the past; don't make me hate you ever, will you?'

She patted his hand that rested on the table, then she walked out of the room. Duffy stood looking at the closed door. Then once more he took off his coat, went over and shot the bolt on the door, kicked off his shoes, and lay down on the bed. He reached up and turned off the light.

In the dark, he lay for a long time thinking. Then he said in a low voice, 'Some nice hot place with plenty of yellow sand. With sky a real blue and just you and me.' He put out his hand to the empty pillow at his side and let his fingers lightly touch the cool linen.

The room felt suddenly cold and empty.

CHAPTER FOURTEEN

Edwin English was a tall, thick-set guy, with a round fleshy face, blue-white hair, and cold, fishy eyes. He sat at a big flat-top desk, a cigar burning slowly in his short white fingers, staring with blank eyes at Duffy.

He sat there for maybe twenty minutes listening to Duffy talk. He examined with no sign of interest the note-book Duffy threw on to the desk. Then he put the cigar back in his mouth and half-closed his eyes. He sat there for some time looking through Duffy at something hanging on the wall behind Duffy's head.

Duffy was satisfied that he had told him everything, concisely and clearly. He thought he had made a swell job of it.

English took the cigar out of his mouth and tapped the top of the desk with a well-manicured finger-nail. 'I could turn you up for a murder rap, it seems,' he said.

Duffy grinned mirthlessly. 'Ain't you working from the wrong angle?' he said. 'You ain't got to worry about me. It's your daughter that you gotta concentrate on.'

English said, 'I'm always concentrating on my daughter.'

Duffy nodded. 'Sure, but not half as hard as you gotta work now. Look, suppose you let me handle this?'

English said, 'You'll be picked up by the police. No, I don't think you would be any good.'

Duffy got to his feet. He still carried the thin smile on his mouth. 'Well, well,' he said, 'I guessed you'd feel like that. If you think I'm taking the rap for her, you got it all wrong. I'm going right down to headquarters and I'm going to squawk so loud you'll hear it right up here.'

English said, 'You haven't got any proof.'

Duffy shrugged. 'That's what you think,' he said. 'I've got enough evidence to get that jane fried three times over.'

English raised his hand. 'Wait,' he said. 'Perhaps we can think up something.'

Duffy came back to the desk. He leant over and stared hard into English's eyes. 'You're playing it wrong. Can't you see how they'd fall over themselves to get Annabel indicted for a first-degree murder rap? They're snapping round your heels already, English, and you know it. One false move from you, and you're out. Your policy ain't popular. I don't like it myself. Let me tell you, it's a goddam awful policy with a daughter like yours around.'

English pushed his chair back and stood up. Just for a second Duffy saw the fishy eyes look uneasy, then they went bland again. Duffy grinned to himself. He knew he had slipped in a hot one.

'What do you propose?' English said.

'Cool the cops off me, for a start. You can do it. Once I've got protection, I can go after Morgan and run him out. I can pick up Annabel and get her into a nut-house . . . that's the place for her.'

English brooded. 'You've got to have more than protection. You want money and you want help.'

Duffy said, 'Gilroy's mob's backing me.'

'Gilroy? Yes, I know him. He's all right, but he's not big enough.'

Duffy sat on the edge of the desk. 'With me around, he'll be big enough.'

'And money?'

'Suppose you put up some dough? It's worth a lot to fix this mess, ain't it?'

English walked to the door. 'We'll see about that,' he said. 'Suppose you come down to headquarters and we'll talk things over with the right man.'

Duffy looked at him hard. He shook his head. 'You gotta fix that,' he said. 'This is too important to me to risk a double-cross. I'd look a grand mug walking into headquarters, if you were losing your grip.'

English shrugged. 'You have a strange way of express-ing yourself,' he said. 'But have it your own way. I'll ring you.'

Duffy looked at the clock on the desk. It was just after eleven o'clock. 'I'll do the ringing. I'll come through after one o'clock. I'll expect to get moving right away by then.'

English nodded, then, as if a thought had struck him, he said, 'Where's Annabel now?'

Duffy shrugged. 'The last time I saw her, she was telling a little nance to shoot me in the guts. You've got a grand daugh-ter, ain't you?'

Leaving English, Duffy picked up the Buick and drove slowly back to the Bronx. He left the car at the garage and then went to his room.

He sent the thin man out to get the newspapers. While he was waiting for them he mixed himself a strong Scotch and lit a cigarette. He let his mind wander as he sat there, but he kept coming back to Olga. He could see her lying naked with the dagger in her breast. He tried to think of other things, but his mind kept switching back to that picture.

He was glad when the thin man came in and dumped several tabloids on the table. Duffy gave him some small change. Then he went through the papers carefully. When he had finished them, he sat back and lit another cigarette. There was nothing in any of the papers about Gleason's murder.

He got up, went to the telephone and dialled Annabel's number. He sat for a minute or so listening to the buzz, and then hung up. Well, anyway, she had skipped all right.

Then he wandered about the room, thinking. He wondered if Morgan's gang had wiped her out and got rid of both bodies.

He thought that was an idea, but he couldn't do anything about that for the moment.

Just before one o'clock, Gilroy came in with two other men. Gilroy said, 'This is Shep,' to Duffy. Duffy looked at Shep and nodded. He thought Shep was an extraordinary-looking man. He had a very small head perched on a long neck, and the rest of his body was grossly fat. His head just didn't fit his body. Duffy thought it looked like the maker of Shep had run out of the right size, and had just slapped on the first head that came to hand. Schultz was a tall, wiry bird, with a thick mop of black hair, that stood up like a wire brush.

Duffy said, 'Sit down, boys, and have a drink.'

They sat down self-consciously, looked at the empty table and then at Duffy. The thin man put his head round the door and Duffy said, 'Let's have some Scotch.'

Gilroy stood by the window. He said, 'I've put the general idea up. They'll go for it okay.'

Shep said in a gritty voice, 'Ain't you the guy the cops are looking for?'

Duffy glanced at Gilroy, who nodded. Then he said, 'That's right, but not for long.' He got up and went over to the telephone and dialled. While he was waiting for the line to connect, the thin man came in with the drinks. Schultz reached out a bony hand and began to fix them.

Duffy said into the 'phone, 'English?' then he said, 'You fixed it yet?'

English said, 'It wasn't easy, but you're in the clear now. You gotta pin this rap on someone, but it's not to be you know who.'

Duffy grinned. 'That's okay. I only want a stiff or two, and that's who's done it.'

English grunted. 'You've got to have your stiffs first,' he said.

'If you could see this outfit sitting right here, you wouldn't worry about that. I want some dough, don't I?'

English said, 'If you run Morgan out and Annabel where I don't have to see her again, you're going to get plenty.'

'It's got to be better than that. I want some on the nail.'

English was silent for a moment. 'I'll open an account for

you at the National. You can draw up to five thousand dollars.'

Duffy said, 'You do that,' and hung up.

Gilroy came over from the window and took a glass from Schultz. He said, 'Let's go.'

Duffy sat down. 'English is covering me. He's lifted the heat for the moment. He'll back me for dough if we give him action. I guess we might start right away.'

Schultz said, 'What's my split?'

'Five grand each,' Duffy said, doing sums in his head.

Shep nodded. 'I could use that,' he said.

'Your first job is to find Annabel English,' Duffy said, folding his arms and resting his elbows on the table. 'That jane is dangerous, and she's got to be put where she won't be.'

Gilroy said, 'Knock her off?' He said it with distaste.

Duffy shook his head. 'I don't want any killings. I can fix her. She's as crazy as a coon.'

Shep said, 'We'll find her, but the nut angle is not up our street.'

Duffy said, 'You find her. I'll do the rest.'

'Where do we start?'

'The last time I saw her, she was with Morgan's mob. They will know what happened to her.'

Shep clambered to his feet. 'That's easy,' he said. 'I know that gang. Leave it to me.'

Duffy waited until he had lumbered out, then he looked at Gilroy. 'Give me the lowdown on Morgan?'

Gilroy said, 'He's running three clubs. He's got offices on Transverse Avenue by the river. That's where he does his business.'

'What business?'

'All his rackets. Calls the place the Morgan Navigation Trust Co. It's his headquarters for vice, smuggling, getting girls over from Cuba, you know the whole works.'

Duffy went over to the book and turned up Morgan Navigation Co. He dialled and waited. Then he said, 'Mr. Morgan there?'

A pert voice said, 'What's it about?'

Duffy said curtly. 'I'll ask him to tell you, if he wants you to know.'

She connected him. Before she plugged, he heard her say, 'Some day these sharp punks will cut themselves with their own wit.'

Duffy grinned. Morgan's voice came over. 'Yes?'

Duffy said, 'Listen, Morgan. Your mob let you down.'

Morgan said very evenly, 'You had the breaks that time, Duffy, but watch out.'

'Gleason's out of the bidding,' Duffy said, looking with blank eyes at the wall in front of him. 'That little book's going to cost you fifty grand.'

He heard Morgan draw his breath in, then he said, 'My boys are collecting that free of charge. I've warned you. They're coming gunning for you.'

Duffy said, 'On second thoughts, I'll turn the book over to the State.'

'I shouldn't do that.' Morgan said it just a little too quickly. There was no punch in the threat.

'I'm turning it over, just the same. Then we'll see what happens. I got twenty-five grand out of Gleason, so I should worry.'

'Wait.' Morgan raised his voice. 'I'll give you five grand.'

Duffy said, 'Make it twenty-five and its yours.'

'Okay,' Morgan's voice was very soft. 'You bring the book over, and I'll have the money here.'

'I'm not that screwy,' Duffy said. 'Turn it over in the open. I'll be in the lobby of the Belmont Plaza at six o'clock tonight. We'll make the exchange.'

There was a short pause, then Morgan said, 'Okay,' and hung up.

Gilroy had been listening, his eyes on Duffy's back. He said, 'You're going to have a sweet time bringing that dough home.'

Duffy picked up his hat. 'Come on,' he said, 'let's go.'

They followed him over to the garage. Duffy said to Schultz, 'Can you handle this bus?'

Schultz nodded. 'You bet,' he said, faintly surprised.

'Well, drive it then. Gilroy and me want to talk.'

Gilroy and Duffy got in at the back and Schultz climbed in under the wheel. 'Where to?' Schultz asked, jerking the starter.

Duffy gave him the address of his bank, and Schultz nosed the car carefully down the narrow alley into the main street.

Duffy said to Gilroy, 'We'll double-cross this louse right away. I'm turning the list over to English and he can get busy on it. It's too big for us to handle. Next, we give the copy to Morgan and get his dough. Then we fix Annabel, and after that we'll call on Morgan's office and collect any evidence to run him out. If we don't turn any up, we'll have to run him out on our own.'

Gilroy leant back against the cushions and closed his eyes. He said sleepily, 'You got quite a programme, ain't you?'

Duffy said, 'I want to get shot of this, then you boys can spend what you've earned.'

Schultz ran the car to the kerb and Duffy went into the bank. The other two stayed in the car, waiting. When Duffy came out he glanced up and down the street, then stepped hastily into the car. Schultz pulled away at once.

Duffy gave English's address. He said, 'Make it fast.' Schultz glanced at him in the driving-mirror, nodded, and swung to the side streets.

Gilroy said, 'Seems a shame to turn that list over to the cops.'

Duffy shrugged. 'You ain't thinking of handling a thing that big?' he asked.

Gilroy shook his head. 'I don't handle dope,' he said. 'I just don't like to give those punks a break.'

Duffy grinned. 'It'll wash up Morgan, so what the hell?'

English was surprised to see him. He took the book from Duffy, glanced at it, then said, 'So this is the first step, eh?'

Duffy nodded. 'You turn that over to the Narcotic Squad. It ain't evidence, but it might stampede some of those hopheads. Anyway, it'll stop Morgan running the same game.'

English nodded. 'Have you found Annabel yet?'

'It won't be long.' Duffy went to the door. 'I'll get in touch pretty soon.'

Out in the street once more, he went over to the Buick. Gilroy said, 'Ain't it time to eat?'

Duffy climbed in. 'Go ahead,' he said. 'I've got time on my hands till six.'

Schultz swung the car in a half-circle, reversed her back again, then spinning the wheel hard round, he turned her completely, heading rapidly east.

CHAPTER FIFTEEN

Shep came in just after five o'clock. Duffy was cleaning his Colt. Gilroy and Schultz sat in chairs, watching him.

Duffy looked up sharply and said, 'Found her?'

Shep waddled in, sat down and blotted his face with his handkerchief. 'Yeah,' he said. 'Guess where?'

Duffy put his gun on the table. His mouth became a thin line. 'Where?' he said.

Shep smiled happily; he said, 'It's rich. She's gone hot pants for Morgan's nance.'

Duffy's eyebrows rose. 'Clive?'

Shep nodded. 'She's over at the little rat's apartment right now. He's in bed, screaming hell, because someone trod on his pan.'

Duffy got to his feet. 'We'll go right over and pick her up,' he said, slipping the gun down his waist-band.

Gilroy said, 'All of us?'

Duffy shook his head. 'Suppose Shep and me go,' he said.

Shep said, 'Sure.' He mumbled something to Gilroy and gave a loud tinny laugh.

Duffy said, 'I'll go on to the Belmont Plaza after. Suppose you two boys get down there and watch the lobby. We ain't going to take any chances with Morgan.'

Gilroy nodded. 'Okay,' he said.

Duffy and Shep went out and climbed in the Buick. Duffy took the wheel. As he pushed the Buick down the street, he said, 'If that jane gets tough, knock her off.'

Shep nodded. 'She's a grand looker, ain't she?' Then he said sadly, 'It's tough being fat.'

Duffy shot him a side-glance. 'You don't know when you're getting the breaks,' he said shortly. 'That jane's poison.'

Shep gave him some directions, then said wistfully, 'I guess it'd be good, going places with a honey like that.'

Duffy said nothing. He drove fast. After a ten-minute run, he said, 'This the street?'

Shep stuck his little head out of the window and peered.

'That's right.'

Duffy drew into the kerb. They both got out. 'What number did you say?'

Shep hunted in his pockets, found a scrap of paper, screwed up his eyes, then said, '1469.'

Duffy checked the house near him. 'It's on the other side farther down.'

Together they crossed the street and began walking casually down. Duffy said, 'They're both dangerous; you got to watch 'em, Shep.'

Shep grinned. 'Me . . . I'm scared to hell . . . like hell,' he said.

1469 was a tall, gaunt apartment house. Duffy ran up the steps and checked the list of names. 'Clive Wessen,' he said. He rang the next bell, waited until the latch gave, pushed open the door and walked in. Shep shuffled behind him. 'Third floor,' Duffy said, keeping his voice down.

They climbed the stairs slowly. The place was clean and bright. Duffy said, 'These punks live well, don't they?'

Shep said nothing, he was saving his breath. On the third floor, Duffy took the Colt out; he held it loosely in his hand, hanging down by his side.

He nodded to a door at the far end of the passage. 'There it is,' he said. 'Can you open it?'

Shep said, 'I can open any door. Watch me.' Moving very quietly, he went to the door, examined the lock, then turned his head and beamed. 'It's a cinch,' he said.

'Get going,' Duffy murmured.

Shep felt in his pocket, took out a little tool, fitted it in the lock and turned. Duffy heard the lock slip with a faint click. He said in Shep's ear, 'Give me two minutes, then come on in.'

Shep nodded and stood aside. Duffy gently turned the handle, pushed open the door, and walked in. He found himself in a small hall, about twelve feet by sixteen. Facing him were two doors. He trod quietly over and listened. He thought he heard someone talking behind the right-hand door. Holding his gun waist-high, he pushed open the door, stepped in quickly. Then he said in a cold voice, 'You seduced him yet?'

Annabel spun round. She was standing by a divan, on which Clive was lying. Clive's face was beautifully bandaged with plaster. Someone had made a very neat job of it. All Duffy could see of Clive's face was two eyes that hated him.

Duffy said very sharply, 'Don't start anything. Keep still.'

Clive said in a curiously adenoidal voice, 'Get out of here.'

Annabel ran her fingers through her hair. She smiled at Duffy. 'I think you're cute,' she said.

Duffy said, 'Sit down.'

Shep wandered in. He looked first at Clive, then at Annabel. He puffed out his cheeks, then took off his hat.

She had sat down on the foot of the divan. She said in her breathless voice, 'Who's your gentleman friend?'

Shep beamed and fingered his necktie. He glanced at Duffy. 'What a honeypot!' he said.

Duffy had his eyes on Clive. Although Clive was dressed, he had a rug over him, hiding his hands. Duffy said, 'Put your hands where I can see them.'

'Suppose we be friends . . .?' Annabel broke in.

Duffy turned his head a little. 'You're coming with me,' he told her. 'We've got a home for you to go to.'

She said, 'Now?'

Duffy said, 'That's it. Right now.'

She stood up. 'Home?' she said suddenly. 'What do you mean . . . home?'

Duffy said, 'You'll know. Say good-bye to your boyfriend, you ain't seeing him any more.'

She looked at Clive, then she shrugged a little. 'I don't mind,' she said. 'He's not quite in one piece. He's a waste of time.'

Shep grinned. 'A jane like you ain't got no right running with a nance,' he said seriously.

Clive said in a low voice, 'Get to hell out of here, all of you.'

Annabel said, 'May I get my things?'

Duffy shook his head. 'You can come as you are,' he said. 'I want to talk to you . . . come on.'

She giggled. 'I love you when you get like that,' she said. 'Let's talk; I've got lots to tell you.' She waved her hand at Clive. 'About him and Morgan. You'll eat it up.'

Clive drew his lips off his teeth, then he shot her. Duffy just caught the slight movement under the rug as the gun roared. The rug began to smoulder.

Duffy fired at Clive, but the big Colt kicked up and the bullet smacked against the wall two feet above Clive's head. Moving with incredible rapidity, Shep flung himself on Clive.

Duffy walked cautiously over to Annabel, looked at her, then shoved his gun in his hip pocket and knelt down beside her. She lay on her back, one hand clenched tightly to her right side. She opened her eyes and looked at him, then she began to cry.

Duffy said, 'Take it easy. You'll be all right.'

He picked her up. Shep said, 'Bring her here.' He had tossed Clive on to the floor. Clive lay flat. Shep had smacked him hard on the chin.

Duffy put her on the divan. He said urgently, 'Get some water and dressing. She's bleeding like hell.'

Shep went out of the room. Duffy could hear him pulling drawers open and hunting about in the next room. He took his pocket-knife and ripped away her clothes round the wound. 'Hurry, damn you,' he shouted to Shep when he saw where she was shot.

Shep came back in a lumbering run. He had a handful of small towels and a jug of water. Duffy took them from him. 'Phone English, and tell him,' he said. 'Get going, this is urgent.'

While he was fixing the wound, she opened her eyes again. She looked at him. She saw the sweat glistening on his face and she said, 'Am I going to die?'

He couldn't do anything to stop the bleeding. He said rather helplessly, 'It's the best way for you, I think.'

She said, 'I think so, too,' and she began to cry again.

He tied a pad over the wound, but he knew it was useless. She said, 'Give me a drink.'

He had to hold her head to give her the Scotch. She said, 'I'm sorry about everything.'

Duffy's face was very hard. 'You little girls are always sorry when it's too late.'

She said, 'It was your fault that I killed your woman.'

Duffy said, 'It's best you should go like this.' He couldn't bring himself to say anything else.

'No other man's ever turned me down,' she said. 'Remember I offered myself?'

'Yeah, I remember. I guessed you'd want to settle that score.'

'If you wrote down everything, I could sign it,' she said. 'I'd like that.'

Duffy took a quick step to the writing-desk, found a pad and came back. She said, in a low voice, 'You'll be quick?'

Duffy said, 'Sure. You killed Cattley, didn't you?'

'Yes, Cattley was double-crossing Gleason, who was my husband. No one knew about that. Gleason was bad, but he was making money. I had to have that. I learnt that Cattley was taking half, so I pushed him down the lift shaft. He was a little man, it was quite easy. You came along and covered me on that. Then Max. You see, they all bothered me. I tried once just to see, but none of them were any good. So after that I didn't want them again. Max was always pressing me. Then he got the photos, and asked me up to his flat to trade them in the usual way, so I went and I killed him too.'

Duffy wrote quickly. He gave her another drink. Shep came in and stood behind him. He said, 'English is coming.' Duffy raised his hand for silence.

Annabel went on, 'I hated you. When I went out to the Shann woman's villa to find the book, I thought you'd both be out. I saw you drive the car away, and I thought she was with you. Then I went inside and she started getting excited, so I killed her too.'

Duffy said, 'It got you nowhere, did it?'

She said, so faintly that Duffy had to lean forward, 'I was so tired of ... Murray ... when you came ... I ... thought I could ... put it ... on you.'

Duffy scribbled quickly, put the pen in her hand. 'Can you do it?' he said anxiously.

She said, 'I . . . can't . . . see.'

Duffy held her hand and put the nib on the paper. 'Sign,' he said loudly and roughly. The pen slipped out of her fingers and her hand dropped out of his. He turned and looked at Shep. 'Can you beat that?' he said savagely. 'This confession lets me out, and I'm damned if she doesn't die on me before she signs.'

Shep said, 'That's tough.'

Duffy stood up. 'Look at her, Shep,' he said. 'You ain't likely to find a worse woman in the country.'

Shep shrugged. 'What's the matter, as long as she looks right?'

Duffy said impatiently, 'Clive okay?'

Shep nodded. 'He'll be out for another hour.'

Duffy glanced at the clock. He saw it was quarter to six. He said, 'Come on, we got a date. Let English fix this.'

Shep followed him out of the apartment and down the stairs. Duffy said when they got into the street, 'Morgan'll just hate me for this.'

Shep grinned as he climbed into the car. 'Yeah,' he said. 'Will they burn the nance?'

Duffy shrugged. 'Maybe English'll hush it all up. But you bet they'll pin something on that nance to keep him busy.'

It was just after six when Duffy swung the Buick to the kerb outside the Belmont Plaza. 'Come with me,' he said.

They walked into the busy lobby. Across the lounge he saw Schultz reading a newspaper. Schultz made no sign that he had seen him, but by the way he folded the paper and laid it down Duffy knew he had.

The little guy and Joe came in. Joe was looking mad, he scowled at Duffy. The little guy said, 'You're going to get into trouble one of these days.'

Duffy said, 'Skip the talk. Let's get down to business.' He walked into the bar. The little guy followed him, leaving Joe in the lobby. Shep beamed at Joe, but said nothing.

The little guy said, when they got to the bar, 'What you doing with Gilroy's mob?'

Duffy stared at him coldly. 'You'll know before long,' he said. 'Come on, let's get this over, you stink.'

The little guy giggled. He put his hand inside his coat and took out an envelope. He opened it and drew out a sheaf of notes. Duffy watched him count them. Twenty-five grand. Then Duffy took the note-book out and they exchanged. The little guy said, 'And the duplicate?' Duffy smiled. His eyes were like ice. 'The State's got that.'

The little guy shook his head sadly. 'You shouldn't have done that,' he said. 'Morgan's going to get mad when I tell him that.'

Duffy said deliberately, 'Morgan can – himself.'

The little guy giggled again. 'I'll tell him that too.' He put the note-book in his pocket. 'Those notes are phoneys,' he said, as an afterthought.

Duffy took the envelope out of his pocket, examined one of the notes carefully. It looked all right to him. 'You don't say,' he said.

The little guy nodded cheerfully. 'Sure, Morgan wouldn't pay a punk like you in real dough.'

Duffy put the notes away. He had an idea.

The little guy said, 'Well, for God's sake, you're taking it quietly, ain't you?'

Duffy said, 'Take my tip, scram.'

The little guy looked at him, then nodded. 'You'll see me again, of course,' he said apologetically.

Duffy said, 'Before you think.'

He watched the little guy walk out, followed by Joe, then he beckoned to Shep and called for two ryes. Shep came over. 'You got it?' he said.

Duffy slipped one of the notes out and gave it to him.

Shep glanced at it, beamed and said, 'As easy as that, huh?'

Duffy pushed the glass over to him, drained his quickly and nodded at the barman. 'One more,' he said.

Shep said, 'You drink too quickly.'

'So long as I don't drink too much, why should I worry?'

Shep frowned, then said, 'It amounts to the same, don't it?'

He gave Duffy back the note reluctantly. Duffy put it with the others. He said, 'Let's go.'

Gilroy and Schultz were sitting in the Buick waiting for them. When the Buick was rolling, Gilroy said, 'No fuss?'

Duffy handed the notes over to him. 'There they are,' he said.

Gilroy counted them and whistled. 'This don't seem natural,' he said.

Duffy stared out of the window. 'Maybe, it ain't.'

Gilroy examined the notes carefully, then he said, 'Phoneys.'

Duffy nodded. 'Yeah, he told me as much before he left.'

'So what?'

Duffy turned his face, so that he looked at Gilroy.

'I guess we're going to frame Morgan with those. It'll be worth twenty-five grand to clap him away. English'll pay as much as that for the job.'

'How . . . frame?'

'We'll go out to his place and plant that stuff tonight. There's a nice little rap for making notes as big as these. Once we get those planted, then we tip English, and he does the rest.'

Gilroy said, 'The dough would've been better.'

Duffy shrugged. 'You can't have everything,' he said.

Shep had been listening to the conversation. He turned his head. 'Say, those notes sure made a sap of me. Why not put 'em on the street? We'd pass 'em okay.'

Duffy said, 'No, that's not the way to play it. You'll get the dough all right, but it'll take a little longer. When you get it, it'll be safe.'

When they got back to the Bronx, Duffy 'phoned English. English said, 'We've got Wessen.'

'How about Annabel?'

'Never mind about her. I've paid another five thousand dollars into your account. That should hold you for a bit.'

Duffy grinned to himself. 'Listen, English,' he said. 'Are you holding Clive Wessen on a murder rap?'

'Murder?' English seemed surprised. 'No, he's in for cocaine smuggling.'

Duffy grinned and winked over his shoulder at Gilroy.

'I bet that guy had his pockets full of the white stuff,' he said.

'The police found enough incriminating evidence to justify an arrest,' English said smoothly.

'I bet they did,' Duffy said. 'And Annabel?'

There was a pause, then English said in a faintly hostile voice, 'You know about that. My unfortunate daughter was killed by a hit-and-run motorist.'

'That's too bad,' Duffy said. 'I'll be having some more work for you in a little while.' He hung up. 'That bird's cagey,' he said to Gilroy. 'They framed Wessen, smothered Annabel's murder. It's a hit-and-run case.'

Gilroy shook his bullet head. 'You gotta watch him.'

Duffy shrugged. 'We're playing on his side.' He went over and helped himself to a drink. 'It's nice to have a guy like that behind you.'

Gilroy nodded and left him. When he had gone, Duffy sat down and did some thinking. Then he got up and went over to the small bureau, unlocked the top drawer, took out the bundle of money he had left there, and looked at it. Then he went to the door and turned the key. He sat down at the table and counted the money carefully. He'd got thirty-four grand and some small notes. He counted on the table three piles of five thousand dollars. That left him nineteen thousand dollars. He split the nineteen grand into four parts. One went into his hip pocket, another in his side pocket, and the third in his trouser pocket. The fourth, three thousand dollars, he folded carefully and put in his shoe. He had to take his shoe off and put it on twice before it was comfortable.

He went over and unlocked the door, picked up the money on the table, and wandered into the bar.

Gilroy was talking to Schultz and Shep. They were drinking beer. They all looked up, a faintly expectant expression on their faces.

Duffy leant on the bar. 'Here's your split,' he said gently. He gave each man the money rolled in a tight ball. 'Five grand,' he said. 'Don't count it now.'

Shep picked up his glass and poured the beer on the floor at his feet. 'Gimme champagne,' he said to the barman. 'I'm goin' to launch myself.'

Schultz fingered his cut, then shoved it in his trouser pocket.

He looked vacantly at Duffy, nodded, and went out.

Gilroy turned his head, watching him walk across the floor. 'That guy's mighty careful with his dough,' he said. 'I wouldn't say he's tight. He's careful.'

Duffy glanced at the clock. 'I'm going to snatch myself a little sleep,' he said. 'We'll get going about eleven.'

Gilroy said, 'Any dough hanging to this job?'

Duffy nodded. 'Sure,' he said. 'I want you boys to make money while you can.'

Shep took his short fat nose out of his glass. 'That's a hell of a way to talk,' he said.

Duffy grinned. 'You expect to earn this dough, don't you?' he said.

'Sure, but we won't work that hard.'

Back in his room, Duffy rang Sam. He said, 'Do you feel like doing me a favour?'

Sam said, 'Aw, forget it, will you? Alice's only a little dumb; she don't know what it is to want things.'

Duffy's mouth twisted. 'You lay off Alice. She's right. See? Alice is goddam right. If I'd got the sense of a louse, I'd be doing a job of work instead of trying to be a big shot. Well, I ain't got the sense, and what's more, I'm getting a kick out of this. What I want you to do is to keep your ear open down at headquarters. I want you to keep an eye on English. That bird's been pulling too many fast ones to make me sleep easy. Will you do that, Sam?'

Sam seemed puzzled. 'Sure,' he said. 'I'll do any little thing like that.'

Duffy said, 'You'll keep me in touch. If anything starts popping, gimme a buzz?'

Sam said, 'Sure,' then he said, 'You know what you're doing?' He sounded worried.

Duffy said, 'I'm bucking something that thinks it's too big for me, but ain't.' He added, ' 'Bye, soldier,' and dropped the receiver on its prong.

Outside, he could hear the rain beating down. He went over to the bed and lay flat, one leg hanging over the side. He scratched the side of his face gently with his nail. 'I wonder . . .' he said to himself, then he heard someone walk past his door.

He heard Gilroy say, 'She don't wear 'em. It saves time.' Shep said something in his tinny voice, but Duffy couldn't hear.

In time, the sound of the rain lulled him.

CHAPTER SIXTEEN

Somewhere a big clock chimed half past twelve as the Buick slid to the kerb. The rain drummed on the roof hard.

Shep said, 'Heck! What a night!'

'You should worry, no one about,' Duffy said, rolling down the window and putting his head out. The rain touched him, cold and sharp. He looked up and down the deserted street, then he rolled up the window again, opened the door, and stepped out. Gilroy followed him.

'Fat, you stay in the car,' Gilroy said.

Shep nodded his tiny head. 'Suits me,' he said. He pulled a Luger from his overcoat pocket and laid it across his knees.

Then Schultz got out. The three hurried across the pavement to a block of offices.

'Round the back,' Duffy said.

They walked on, turned a narrow alley, and then stopped. Just above their heads was the fire-escape. Gilroy put his back against the wall, folded his hands in front of him, and nodded at Schultz. Schultz put his foot in Gilroy's cupped hands, and Gilroy hoisted him up. Schultz just touched the fire-escape with his fingers. He said, 'Higher.'

Gilroy gave a little grunt, shifted his feet and raised Schultz a few inches. Schultz's fingers curled on the iron rung, and then he put his weight on it. The fire-escape creaked and slowly came down.

Duffy went up first, then Gilroy, then Schultz. On the first landing, Duffy stood aside, whilst Schultz opened a window. He did it very easily. They all climbed into a dark corridor.

Duffy said, 'It's on the first floor.'

They walked quietly forward, Duffy a little ahead, the other two on either side of him, a few steps in the rear. Duffy held a powerful flash directed on the floor. He kept the beam down, but the reflection lit up the frosted panelled doors. At the end of the corridor Duffy read, 'Morgan Navigation Trust Co.'

'Here,' he said.

Schultz examined the lock, bent over it, then stepped back. He said in a low voice, 'Go ahead.'

Duffy pulled the Colt from his waist-band and gently opened the door. Then he walked in.

The office was big. Steel files lined the walls. There were three large flat-topped desks. Three typists' desks, holding typewriters. The centre desk had a number of telephones.

Duffy said, 'Morgan's room is over there, I guess.'

He wandered over to a door at the far end of the office and went through. The room was smaller than the outer office, but it was more luxurious.

Duffy went round the desk and sat down. He tried the drawers, but they were all locked. He looked over at Gilroy. 'I guess we won't disturb anything. Morgan might tumble. I'll just plant the notes and we'll blow.'

Schultz said, 'Maybe there's a heap of dough in this joint.' He said it wistfully.

Duffy took the roll of counterfeit money from his pocket, spread them flat. He leant forward, picked up a framed calendar and took off the back. Then he put the notes in the calendar and replaced the back.

'You like that?' he said.

Gilroy nodded. 'That'll be difficult to find.'

'You'll be surprised.' Duffy pulled the telephone towards him and dialled a number.

While the line buzzed, the three stayed motionless. Only Gilroy showed he was anxious. His big eyes rolled continuously.

The line connected. English said, 'Who's that?' He sounded sharp.

Duffy drawled into the 'phone, 'I've got Morgan sewed up,' he said. 'If your boys make a call at his office early tomorrow, they can safely slap a charge on him.'

'Where are you?'

'It don't matter. Look, this is a tip off. Morgan's got twenty-five grand in phoney notes hidden in his desk calendar. Could you make that stick?'

English was silent for a moment, then he said, 'You certainly get action, don't you? We'll make it stick all right.'

Duffy said, 'Morgan Navigation Trust Co.'

'I know.' English hung up gently.

Duffy pushed the telephone away from him and stood up. 'Let's go,' he said.

They walked out of the office, carefully relocking the door, down the fire-escape, into the pouring rain.

Shep was still sitting there, fondling his gun. They climbed into the Buick, and Schultz started the engine.

Shep said, 'All right?'

'Easy,' Duffy returned, lighting a cigarette. 'Morgan's going to get a mighty big shock tomorrow.'

Gilroy said out of the dark, 'English has got to be pretty leery to pin anything on that bird.'

Duffy forced a thin stream of smoke down his nostrils. 'English can handle him all right,' he said. 'You see.'

Schultz said, 'We go back, don't we?'

Duffy nodded. 'Yeah,' he said, 'the hay wants hitting.'

As Schultz headed East, Shep said in a confidential whisper to Duffy, 'I thought I'd have a woman tonight. You know, just to celebrate the five grand.'

Duffy nodded sleepily. He began to think about Olga.

'It's a hell of a night to look for a woman, ain't it?' Shep went on gloomily.

Duffy grunted. He wished Shep would shut up.

Schultz had been listening. He said, 'For God's sake, Fat, what you want with a woman?'

Shep giggled self-consciously, and Gilroy joined in. 'He's got the dough, why shouldn't he enjoy himself? Lay off him,' he said.

They drove two blocks in silence, then Shep said to Duffy, 'Ain't you got a woman?'

Duffy turned his head slightly. He could just see Shep's face, stuck like a turnip on his shoulders, as the street lights flashed past, lighting Shep at regular intervals. 'Think about your own troubles,' his voice was cold. 'I'll think about mine.'

'You bet,' Shep said hastily. 'I didn't mean a thing.'

Gilroy broke in, 'Did English say anything about dough, when he talked to you?'

Duffy shook his head, then remembering that Gilroy couldn't see him, he said, 'No.'

The Buick ran along the kerb, slowed, and came to a stop outside the Bronx.

Schultz said. 'Hop out. I'll take her over to the garage.'

They climbed out and hurried down the basement steps, the rain beating down on them.

Gilroy unlocked the door and they entered quickly. The passage was dark. Gilroy swore softly. 'Where the hell's Jock got to?' he said, speaking of the thin man. 'He ought to be still up.'

'Maybe he's got himself drunk,' Shep said. 'I gave him ten bucks out of my split.'

Gilroy groped around and switched on the light. 'You come and have a drink?' he said to Duffy.

Duffy said, 'Sure, my feet are wet. I could do with a shot of Scotch.'

Gilroy led the way down the passage, and walked into the bar. The first thing that caught his eye was the thin man. He was lying on his back, his hands and legs sprawling and his face a mask of blood.

The little guy said sharply, 'Reach.'

Gilroy and Duffy raised their hands. Shep dropped on his knee, drew his Luger and fired at the little guy all in one movement.

Joe, stepping behind the door, tapped Shep with the butt of his gun as he fired. Shep gave a little cough and fell on his hands and knees. He looked like a stricken elephant.

Duffy said between his teeth, 'Don't touch him again.'

Joe looked at him in wonder, then he grinned. 'My, ain't you a pip?' he said admiringly.

The little guy said apologetically, 'Take it easy. Don't move. I'd hate to pop this heater, but I gotta do it if you crowd me.'

Gilroy said, hardly moving his rubbery lips: 'What you want?'

'We want the pip,' Joe said. 'Ain't he hung a rap on Clive?

Well, sure we want the pip. I wanta bounce him a little, don't I?' He looked triumphantly at the little guy. Then he walked over to Duffy, grinning from ear to ear. He feinted with his left, and hit Duffy on his ear, with a tremendous swinging punch that started from his ankles.

Duffy saw it coming a split second too late. A bomb burst inside his head. A bright light blotted the room out.

'Spill his guts,' the little guy said with a snigger. 'Go on, Joe, burst him open.'

Joe walked over to Duffy quickly with long, sliding steps. He put his hand down on Duffy's body, seized Duffy low and swung him off the floor. He lifted him quite easily and smashed him down on the boards, as if he were dumping coal.

The little guy said, 'Let's get him out of here.'

Joe said, 'Sure.' He dragged Duffy to his feet and began pulling him to the door.

Gilroy stood like a waxwork, only his great eyes rolling in terror. The little guy looked at him, curling up his tight mouth. 'Here it is, nigger,' he said, and squeezed the trigger. The gun crashed. Gilroy stood with his hands folded over his belly, gradually sinking at the knees. His curiously coffee-coloured skin glistened with sweat. He went down very slowly. First on his knees, then a little on one side. His hip-bone struck the floor hard, and his face followed, cutting the flesh on the boards.

The little guy stood over him, looking at Joe. 'Shall I finish him?' he asked.

Joe paused in the doorway, holding Duffy by his shirt-front. 'Let the punk bleed,' he said, with a snarl. 'It takes longer that way, don't it?'

The little guy giggled and pushed his gun back in his holster. 'You get ideas,' he said.

Joe admired himself. 'Don't I?' he said, walking down the passage, pulling Duffy with him. He said over his shoulder, 'I'm going to give myself a grand time with this bum.'

The little guy followed him closely. He opened the front door, and together they stepped out into the driving rain.

The sudden cold driving shower of water brought Duffy to his senses. He placed his legs firmly against the step and arched his body. Joe was brought up short. He swore at Duffy, who swung a punch blindly into the darkness. He hit Joe on the nose. He so startled Joe that the big tough let him go and reeled back, took a false step and almost went over.

Duffy scrambled away hastily, just as Schultz began blazing away from across the road. Schultz's .45 roared three times. Duffy felt a slug thud into the wall above his head.

The little guy fired twice at Schultz, his gun cracking like dry wood snapping, only much louder. Duffy fumbled at his waist, and pulled out his Colt. He crouched in the shadow, trying to see where Joe was. The rain blinded him, and the solitary street light, about fifty feet away, threw only black shadows.

Holding the gun, Duffy began to back further into the dark. He wanted to cross the road and get over to Schultz. Further down the road, the blackness was intense. He thought, if he could get there, he could cross in safety. He felt his heart beating hard against his ribs, but he wasn't scared. He felt a strong sense of exhilaration flooding through him.

Schultz began firing again. Three sharp sounds. Duffy could see the flash from the gun. He crossed the road, running bent double.

Faintly, somewhere at the far end of the street, came the faint blast of a whistle, then a low drumming of a nightstick being beaten on the pavement.

Schultz called to him, 'The cops.'

Duffy ran forward again, keeping to the wall, hugging the dark shadows. Schultz from a doorway pulled him into the shelter.

He said, 'I've got to get out of here quick. The bulls know me.'

Duffy said, 'Gilroy's dead.' He spoke as if he had been running a long way. 'The cops can't touch you. I've got protection.'

Schultz snarled in the darkness. 'My rod's hot,' he said.

Duffy held out his hand. 'Change,' he said. 'They won't look at mine.'

Schultz passed his over, and took Duffy's. They heard the wail of a siren, and a fast, closed car came swinging round the corner. Duffy stepped out into the street and waved. The car skidded to a standstill.

Four beefy faces looked at him from the car, suspiciously. He felt the hidden menace of guns, unseen in the dark, threatening him. He stood quite still.

Then one of them said, 'It's okay. I know this guy.'

Duffy stepped up to the car. 'Morgan's gang've just knocked Gilroy off,' he said slowly, putting his foot on the step. 'I was there. You've come along at the right time.'

Hesitatingly, three of the cops got out of the car and stood undecided in the rain, then they turned and walked over to the Bronx.

Duffy jerked his hand, signalling to Schultz, and followed them. Schultz, walking with elaborate caution, crossed the road and caught up with Duffy.

Inside, the three cops stood and looked at Gilroy, then walked over and stirred Shep with a foot.

One said, 'He'll be okay. Just a rap.'

The Sergeant caught sight of Schultz, and his face clouded. Duffy could see the sullen hostile expression blotting out indifference. The Sergeant said, 'Where were you?'

Duffy broke in, 'He's okay. He was putting my car away.'

The Sergeant looked at Duffy, scowled, then said, 'You're in the clear now, but watch your step.' There was an ominous threat in his voice. It puzzled Duffy.

Shep began to move. Straightening his great limbs, and grunting. He raised his head painfully. Duffy thought he looked like a stranded turtle, lying there.

He said, 'It's all right.'

Shep looked at him blankly, sat up and rubbed the back of his head. He began to swear softly and vilely. When he saw Gilroy, he stopped. He turned his head and looked at Duffy. Then he got to his feet.

The Sergeant had given instructions for an ambulance; he was wandering round the room, sniffing suspiciously at everything.

Duffy said to Shep, 'They beat it in the rain.'

Shep put his hand across his eyes and squeezed his temples, as if trying to force his eyes back to normal. He said in his tinny voice, very low and hoarse, 'I'll square those rats, you see.'

Schultz was watching the cops uneasily. He said out of the corner of his mouth, 'These birds ain't acting friendly.'

Duffy went across the room and fixed drinks. He said, 'You boys want something while you're waiting?'

The two cops looked up, their stupid faces brightening. The Sergeant said, 'Skip that. You know better.'

Duffy held the glass in his hand, astonished, but he said nothing. The ambulance came up then. They could hear the siren, and two white-coated attendants scooped Gilroy up and took him away.

The Sergeant came over to Schultz. 'You got a rod?' he said.

Schultz pulled Duffy's Colt from his holster and handed it over. The Sergeant examined it, his eyes narrowed, and his lips thin red. 'We'll look this over,' he said. 'It might have a record.'

Duffy moved forward and took the gun out of the Sergeant's hand. He said in a hard voice, 'Tell English I took it from you,' he said. 'I want this cannon for a while.'

Thick red veins knotted at the Sergeant's neck. His watery blue eyes bulged. He didn't say anything, but walked out, jerking his head at the other two.

When they had gone, Schultz said uneasily, 'Those guys seem to hate us.'

Duffy stood frowning at the floor. Then he said, 'I don't like this. Maybe English's losing his grip.'

He went to his room and dialled. When English answered, Duffy said, 'We've had a shooting here.' His voice was tense and sharp. 'Morgan's mob knocked off Gilroy and tried to iron me out. They got away.'

English said, 'You got to be careful.'

Duffy grinned mirthlessly at the mouthpiece. 'You telling me,' he said. 'What I want you to know is the cops seemed kind of unfriendly. You're giving me protection. I don't like to have it come back on me. These birds were only keeping their hands off me with an effort.'

English said softly, 'You're wanted for a murder rap. You can't expect too much.'

Duffy stared at the opposite wall. 'How long's your protection going to last, once Morgan's out of the way?'

English said immediately, 'You've got nothing to worry about. I'm getting the papers to run the whole case tomorrow, clearing you. You see, you'll be in the clear tomorrow.'

Duffy said, 'We've fixed Morgan. You'll pay twenty-five grand into my bank tomorrow?'

English said, 'Sure, tomorrow. When they got Morgan I'll do that.'

Duffy said, ' 'Bye,' and hung up. He walked across to the window and looked out, lifting the blue blind away from the window. He could only see faintly the street light. He dropped the blind and went once more to the telephone. It began to ring. Its sudden violence startled him. He sat on the edge of the bed and pulled the receiver towards him.

Alice's voice said, 'Oh, Bill.'

He said, 'Why, for God's sake. It's nearly two o'clock. What makes you call at this time?'

She said, her voice uneven, 'Sam just heard .They say there's been shooting at the Bronx. I was so frightened. I thought something had happened to you.'

'Where's Sam?'

'They called him up. He's gone down to headquarters. You are all right?'

'Sure, I'm all right. There's nothing to worry about.' He paused and then went on, 'Listen, honey, you're right. This is getting me nowhere. I'm quitting. I got nineteen grand salted away, and another little packet tomorrow, then I'm through. English is taking the heat off, and it's going to turn out swell.'

She said, 'I . . . I'm glad. It *is* all right, isn't it, Bill?' He thought she was crying.

'You see,' he said, 'tomorrow we'll have a party. You and Sam and me. It's going to be fine. And listen, I'm coming round in the afternoon, and you and me will go shopping. You can buy yourself the world. Doll yourself up and surprise Sam. How do you like that?'

She said, her voice still anxious, 'I shan't rest until you're with us.'

'Good night,' he said .'You're worrying about nothing.'

When he hung up, he sat on the edge of the bed thinking. A little shiver ran through him suddenly, and he got up impatiently. 'Hell,' he said. 'I guess my feet *are* damp.'

CHAPTER SEVENTEEN

Duffy woke with a start. Across the room, the sun leaked round the side of the blind, throwing ragged lines of light on the walls.

The telephone was ringing, grinding shrilly.

He said, 'Goddam it,' and turned over in the bed. Pulling the blanket over his ears, he tried to ignore the jarring noise, but the bell went on ringing, insistently.

He turned over again and climbed stiffly out of the bed. Scooping up the telephone, he shouted, 'What the hell is it?'

Sam was yelling at the other end. He was so excited that Duffy couldn't understand a word. He said, 'I can't hear you. What is it?'

Sam choked, then came over quieter. 'For God's sake, Bill,' he said. 'Hell's broken loose this end. English's double-crossing you. He's slapped every rap he can lay hold on you.'

Duffy stiffened. 'Tell me,' he said.

'They arrested Morgan on some counterfeit charge. Then English got on to headquarters and withdrew his protection. I was there when he did it. He's thrown you to the wolves. They're indicting you for Olga's, Gleason's and Annabel's murder.'

Duffy sat limply on the bed, still holding the telephone. 'The lousy rat,' he said.

Sam said urgently, 'You've got to go carefully. They can't hope to make all those raps stick.'

Duffy's mouth twisted. 'They'll carry me to the station, that it?'

Sam said, 'English is pulling wires. They're waiting for you to run, then they'll come after you with gunpowder.'

'That'll let English right out of this, won't it? Me stiff, he can pin all his lousy scandal to my tombstone.'

'What the hell are you going to do?'

Duffy said, 'Skip, I guess I might make it in the Buick.'

Sam said, 'They'll be watching your joint by now. The news came over ten minutes ago. They started right away.'

Duffy said, 'Do they know you're in this?'

'No. They don't even know I know you.'

'If I can't make it, can I hide up at your place?'

'Sure,' Sam spoke without hesitation. 'Why not come on over and lay up, until the heat's cooled?'

'I'll try a getaway first.' Duffy said gently, 'Thanks, soldier, you've been a swell help. My love to Alice. Don't tell her more than you need.' He hung up and looked quickly at the clock. It was just after ten o'clock.

He dressed with cold unhurried haste. He made sure that he had his money safely distributed in his pockets, then picking up his hat he walked to the door, shot the bolt and stepped quietly into the passage.

As he walked into the deserted bar, he heard the faint wail of a siren, approaching rapidly. He smiled, without being amused, turned back and ran to the front door. He stepped into the street and walked across the road fast, but without any panic. He walked like a man about to start a day's work, who knows he's a little behind the clock.

He could see a long closed car swinging round the bend at the far end of the road. The siren was silent. He stepped hastily into the shadow of the garage and walked over to the Buick.

Schultz said, 'Wait!' His voice had an edge to it.

Duffy peered and saw him standing in the dim light, half hidden by a big Packard.

'The cops are moving in,' Duffy said in a low voice. 'I'm skipping. Want to come?'

Schultz shook head. He was standing very still. Duffy looked again, then stiffened. Schultz was holding a shotgun in his hands; he was pointing it directly at Duffy.

Duffy said with stiff lips, 'What's the idea?'

'Put that dough on the floor,' Schultz said, 'then you can skip.'

Duffy said, 'The cops are just across the road. You can't start anything.'

Schultz's face was white, beads of sweat stood out on the backs of his hands. He said, 'Don't talk. Put the dough down quick.'

Duffy slowly put his hand inside his coat. The Colt-butt felt cold under his touch. Something was forcing him to pull that gun. A hidden instinct to keep what was his. His fingers closed over the butt and he braced himself. Then he jerked at the butt, at the same time he threw himself to one side.

There was a sharp choked roar from the shotgun, and something bit into Duffy's side, sending him over on the oily concrete. White-hot wires of pain shot to his brain, making him feel sick and dizzy. He couldn't think of anything, just the jagged pain eating at his chest.

Faintly he heard someone cursing him, and then hands roughly jerked him this way and that. When the blinding light went away from his eyes, he saw Schultz run out of the garage, holding a gun tightly in his hand.

Duffy pulled himself to his feet by holding on to the wing of the Packard. He heard Schultz fire once, then twice. The noise of Schultz's gun was followed by a sharper report, as the cop in the car began shooting. The other cops were still in the Bronx.

Walking unsteadily over to the Blick, Duffy got in and started the engine. He tasted blood on his tongue, and he began to cough. Hard, tearing cough, that made his brain rattle in his skull. He could feel the blood running down his side, down his leg, into his shoe. Holding hard on to the wheel, he started the engine, slammed in the gear and shot out into the road. Schultz was still firing carefully at the cop from behind a stationary car. As Duffy swept past, both the cop and Schultz fired at him. The bullets made a cobweb on the window, but that was all. In his driving-mirror, he saw Schultz suddenly throw up his hands, and go over, like the felling of a tree. He had no time to see anything else, as the main road was ahead of him.

He drove fast, holding the wheel in both hands very hard, and sitting forward, his back clear of the seat. Hammers beat inside his head, and his chest seemed as if someone were stripping the flesh off his bones. He bit on to his underlip, and drove. His one fixed thought was to get to Sam's place. It wasn't far and it was safe. He thought if he held on a little longer, he'd make it.

Twisting and doubling, he felt that he had shaken off pursuit for the moment. The cop in the car hadn't much chance, with Schultz blazing away at him, to spot the Buick's plates. Anyway, that was what Duffy hoped. He came to McGuire's apartment round the back, pulling up in the narrow alley that skirted the fire-escapes from the block.

He felt strangely hot and weak, sitting there, and he wondered how the hell he was going to get up to the apartment. His wound seemed to have stopped bleeding now, and he looked down at the blood-caked suit with a little grimace. Then he reached over the back of the car and pulled his light dust-coat off the back seat. The effort made the sweat start out all over him, and he had to shut his eyes, as the building reeled drunkenly before him. He sat like that for several moments, then he began to cough again. Deep, tearing coughs that hurt.

It took him a long time to open the heavy door. He was surprised to find how weak he was. Then he stepped to the ground and immediately fell on his knees. He pulled himself up by the door, swearing softly. Obscene words, lodged deep in his subconscious, came tumbling from his lips. He steadied himself and put on the coat, hiding his bloodstained suit. Then he began to walk with uneven, hurried steps round the front.

He had to stop three times before he made it, but he got into the automatic elevator, shut the gates, pressed the button, and folded up on the floor.

The cage groaned and creaked on its upward journey. Duffy just sat there on the floor, breathing with little short gasps, frightened of the pain when he breathed normally. The elevator came to rest after an interminable time. He pulled himself to his feet by hooking his fingers in the grille. He stayed there, hanging on, like a man uncertain of his strength, breasting a gale. Then he balanced himself on the balls of his feet and took away his hands. Pulling open the grille, he lurched into the corridor.

Across the way was McGuire's apartment. He shuffled over

and rapped on the door. Almost immediately Alice came. Her
face lit up when she saw who it was, but almost at once her
expression changed to alarm. 'Bill, what is it?'

Before he could speak, the cough caught him again, and he
folded up, his shoulder against the door.

She said, 'O God,' very softly, and put her arm round him,
pulling him inside. She thrust the door to with her foot, and
supported him through the sitting-room, into the bedroom.

He said thickly, 'The flowers look good.'

She lowered him to the bed, putting a pillow under his head.
'What is it?' she asked.

'Get me a drink, honey,' he mumbled, his mouth suddenly
very dry.

Unsteadily, she ran into the other room, and returned with a
bottle and glass. She poured him a stiff whisky, and held his
head while he drank. The spirit knitted his will, and he managed to grin.

'Get my things off, baby,' he said. 'I ran into a handful of
slugs.'

Undressing him took time. She had to let him rest every
now and then, but she finally got down to his shirt, and the
caked blood nearly made her faint. Duffy said, 'Don't get
scared.' He felt a lot stronger. 'I don't think it's bad. It just
hurts a lot.'

She ran into the bathroom and came back with dressing,
water and towels. She had to cut away his shirt. He had six
pellet-holes down his right side. They had ceased to bleed. She
stood looking at them, her eyes big and scared.

He said, 'Listen, baby. You gotta get them out.'

'I can't,' she said. 'I don't know how.'

'Got some tweezers? You fix your eyebrows, don't you?' His
mouth twisted into a little grin. 'Try with those.'

She looked at him, and shook her head.

He said, 'It's important, baby.'

When he said that, she drew a sharp breath and went over to
the dressing-table. He reached for the bottle and gave himself a
long pull.

She came back, holding the tweezers.

He said, 'Burn a match round 'em.'

While she was doing that, he drank some more whisky. By the time she started on him, he was pretty high.

Wires of pain clutched him, and sweat ran down his face. But he lay quite still, with his eyes shut, giving no sign that she hurt him.

He heard her say at last, 'I've got them all.' She sounded so far away that he turned his head slowly and looked at her. She was white, her large eyes sunk far in her head. Holding on to the edge of a small table, she seemed to sway before his eyes.

He said, 'Get a grip on yourself.' He tried to speak sharply, but just couldn't make it. 'Have a quick drink, you're going to faint or something.'

She sat down on the floor. 'I'll ... be ... all right,' she said, forcing her head down. 'Don't worry. Just ... give me a minute.'

With a shaking hand he slopped some whisky into the glass and thrust it at her. 'Go on, drink it,' he said. The effort made his head swim.

He heard the glass rattle against her teeth as she drank. Then she got up unsteadily and put the glass on the table. 'I'm all right now,' she said.

Duffy said, 'Put some dressing on this, and let me lie easy.'

She sat down on the bed. 'Would it be safe to get a doctor?'

He shook his head. 'No, I'm on the run now, baby.'

She began cutting a pad, biting her lips to stop her tears. He lay on his back, staring at the ceiling, slightly dazed by the alcohol.

She said, 'I'll fix it with tape.'

Duffy said, 'You're swell.'

With inexperienced hands, she strapped him, making a fair job of it. He lay watching her, and when she was done, he said, 'Get me one of Sam's suits.'

Her eyes opened. 'What do you mean?'

'I'm getting out of here.'

'Oh no, you're not,' she said; 'you're staying.'

He shook his head impatiently. 'I ain't getting you mixed up in this. There's a rap for you, if they find me here.'

She said, with determination, 'Don't get tough. You're staying.'

He shut his eyes. 'Okay,' he said weakly. 'Just for a little while.'

She bent over and kissed his hot forehead. 'I'm so sorry,' she said.

He lifted his lids with an effort. 'I started this . . . I guess it had to finish like this.' Then, remembering, he said urgently, 'Look in my coat. There ought to be some dough there.'

She went over and gingerly examined the coat. 'Nothing here,' she said.

His mouth twisted 'Schultz got it,' he said. The effort to worry was too much for him, and he closed his eyes.

She said, 'Try and sleep.'

'My right shoe. There's three grand hidden in it. It's for you.'

She said, 'Never mind that.'

He raised his head, his eyes feverishly on her face.

'Take my shoe off and get the dough,' he said urgently. 'It's all I got out of this mess . . . it's for you.'

She undid his shoes and took them off. She found the crumpled notes wedged in one of them. Holding the little ball of money in her hand, she stood there, tears running down her face.

He dropped his head back on the pillow again. 'You're right, baby,' he said slowly. 'Money don't mean a thing.'

She said, keeping her voice steady, 'I'll leave you now. You must sleep. If you want me, call. I'll be right outside.'

He said drowsily, 'Sure, don't get Sam. I'm going to be okay. I'm feeling fine, only tired.'

She pulled a light blanket over him, and he reached out and took her cool hand. 'I've been a mug,' he said.

Alice clenched her teeth hard to stop the sob that rose in her throat. She looked down at his white, drawn face, and forced her trembling lips into a smile. 'You . . . you're okay now,' she said. 'Forget about it. You see, it's going to be all right.'

She left him lying there on the bed. The heat of the street filtering through the window made him feel heavy and lifeless. The throb in his side was not bad. He just wanted to sleep.

How long he slept, he never knew. It might have been a few minutes, or a few hours, but he woke suddenly, his brain clear and full of strange urgent alarms. He raised his head and looked round the room, then over to the window. When his eyes reached the square of glass, he knew why he had awakened.

Joe and the little guy were standing on the fire escape, watching him. Even as he saw them, Joe pushed up the window, and stepped into the room. He said in a low voice, 'We saw the bus, so we just dropped in.'

The little guy sat on the sill. He nodded at Duffy. 'We've been looking for you,' he said.

Duffy turned his eyes to the door. 'You wouldn't hurt her?'

Joe showed his teeth. 'Not if she stays out,' he said, keeping his voice down, 'but if she comes in, she'll get a surprise.'

Duffy dropped his head back on the pillow. He said, 'Lock the door.'

The little guy said, 'Leave it, Joe. He won't squawk if she can get in easily.' He smiled at Duffy, a tight little smile.

Joe wandered over to the bed and jerked off the blanket His brutish face lit up when he saw the strapping. 'You hurt?' he said. 'Ain't that too bad.'

Duffy said nothing; he just fixed Joe with hot, burning eyes. Whatever Joe did to him, he musn't let Alice hear.

Joe reached out a hand. Duffy stiffened, then realizing how futile it was, just kept his eyes on Joe's face. Joe took the pad in his fist, and ripped it and the strapping away.

The little guy giggled.

Duffy sank his teeth into his lower lip. He was very pale. The six little wounds began to ooze blood, running down Duffy's ribs on the sheet.

Joe sat down on the bed beside him. 'Listen, pip,' he said. 'First you got Clive, then you fixed Morgan. You got a lot coming to you, ain't that right?'

Duffy said through his clenched teeth, 'Go ahead . . . only quickly.'

The little guy said, 'Yes, Joe – get going.'

Joe said, 'I wanta take this guy apart an' see what makes him tick.'

'That jane'll be in,' the little guy said.

Joe grimaced. 'I'll spill her insides all over this punk,' he said.

Duffy lay flat on his back, looking up at the ceiling. His face and chest glistened with sweat. He was afraid, not for himself, but for Alice.

Joe put his big hand on Duffy's throat and squeezed. The little guy got off the window-sill and came over to watch. His mouth hung open a little. He stood on the far side of the bed, his eyes screwed up, watching.

Joe said, 'Have a little air, lug,' and eased the pressure, then he tightened his grip again.

The little guy suddenly cocked his ear. He said, 'Listen.'

Joe sat very still. His hand slightly relaxed. The only sound was the soft thrashing of Duffy's legs on the bed. A muscular reaction he had no control over. From the other side of the door they could hear Alice moving about, and they could hear the faint sound of crockery being moved.

'She's getting him a meal,' the little guy said.

Joe grinned. 'He's losing his appetite, ain't you, bright boy?' The effort of keeping his grip tight was making his face a little red. Then, drawing his lips back in a snarl, he threw his weight on his arms, savagely squeezing.

The little guy moved restlessly from one foot to the other. The room was absolutely silent now, except for Joe's heavy breathing. Then Joe got off the bed, flexing his thick fingers.

The little guy stepped to the window, then he jumped back quickly. 'Joe—'

Forms darkened the window, as three policemen, guns in hands, raced up the fire escape. They slipped into the room with paralysing speed.

Joe stood there, his mouth open, and the whites of his eyes suddenly yellow with terror. 'Don't you shoot,' he said with a jerk, putting up his hands.

The Sergeant pushed forward. His small eyes startled. 'Quite a party,' he said.

The little guy giggled. He stood close against the wall, his hands high. 'You ain't got nothing on us,' he said through white lips.

The Sergeant walked over to the bed, and stood looking. The other two officers remained motionless, their guns menacingly still.

The Sergeant said, 'Well, for God's sake.'

He walked over to the little guy and hit him in the middle of his face with his gun butt. The little guy's head thudded against the wall, and his legs spread, sliding him to the floor. He put his hands over his face, but he couldn't make a sound; he seemed to go into a fit.

Joe buckled at the knees. 'Okay, boss,' he quavered. 'We didn't mean anything by it.'

The Sergeant hunched his shoulders. 'Sure, you didn't, you dirty rat,' he said. 'I've been waiting to nail you for a long time. Well, you've got it coming to you.' He jerked his head to the other two. 'Get the bums outa here.'

Just then the door jerked open, and Alice stood there. The Sergeant stepped in front of her, and crowded her into the kitchen. She retreated, her eyes growing big.

She said, 'You can't take him away ... he's too ill ... Please ...'

The Sergeant said, 'That guy on the bed – Duffy?'

Alice nodded dumbly. 'He's been shot ... he's bad ... please leave him there. Look, I'm getting him some soup. It's ready ... you'll let him have that?'

The Sergeant pushed his cap to the back of his head, and blew out his cheeks. Her terrified face embarrassed him. 'It don't matter about the soup,' he said. He fumbled with his gun, pushing it into his hip pocket. Then he added, 'He won't need it now.'